A War of

Volume One of Book One

of

The Anura Chronicles

Samuel A. Zamor

A WAR OF STONES AND SCALES
Volume 1 of Book 1
First Edition

For mom, dad, Andrew, Oscar, Urga, Tim and everyone else who believed in me.

Dear reader,

I love dragons! I always have! That's why I decided to write about a dragon civilization! You're about to see and experience dragons in a way you've never before and that media has never portrayed.

You hold in your hands a work that has been ruminating and slowly marinating in the fire for over a decade. I started drafting this crazy dragon story back in 2012-2013 when I was 15-16 years old in high school. It's lived with me for almost half my life, I see dragons in my waking hours and their wings keep me warm as I sleep in the recesses of my dreams, where my passion is truly kindled to burn in the eternal fires of my imagination.

It took eight years to draft this story and two to edit. All the characters are dear to my soul, and I know them all, their hopes, dreams, dark sides, flaws and personalities like the back of my hand. I've spent immeasurable hours with them and in their minds. I hope they form an everlasting impression on you, your mind and that maybe you'll find parts of yourself in them as well. Reality inspires fiction and vice-versa, right?

I hope you enjoy this story and all the passion, time, dedication and energy that went into this world to bring it to you, dear reader.

I present to you part 1 of 4 of book 1 of my world!

Welcome to my dragon civilization! May you fly high and not get burned!

A note to readers

This is Volume 1 of A War of Stone and Scales, Book 1 of The Anura Chronicles.

The entire book is comprised of 4 volumes, each of which have been completed. I will be releasing each of these subsequent volumes every 6-8 months. The reason for this primarily being production delays and me being reasonable and not wanting to force-feed a 930 pg and 243K word debut novel onto people who don't know me. I understand that expecting you to read a book of that magnitude by an unknown and totally new author is quintessentially the epitome of pretentiousness and aloof facetiousness. And we can't have that, at least not starting out anyways! Maybe later.

That being said, part 1 is rather short. Just over 200 pages. It's enough to be read in a few hours or a leisurely afternoon at best.

I appreciate you choosing to embark on this epic journey with me.

Lastly, if you ever have difficulty pronouncing the names of characters and places or stumble upon new and unfamiliar words, phrases and terminologies, as you undoubtedly will, please refer to the glossary of terms at the back.

Enjoy!

Contents

Illustrations

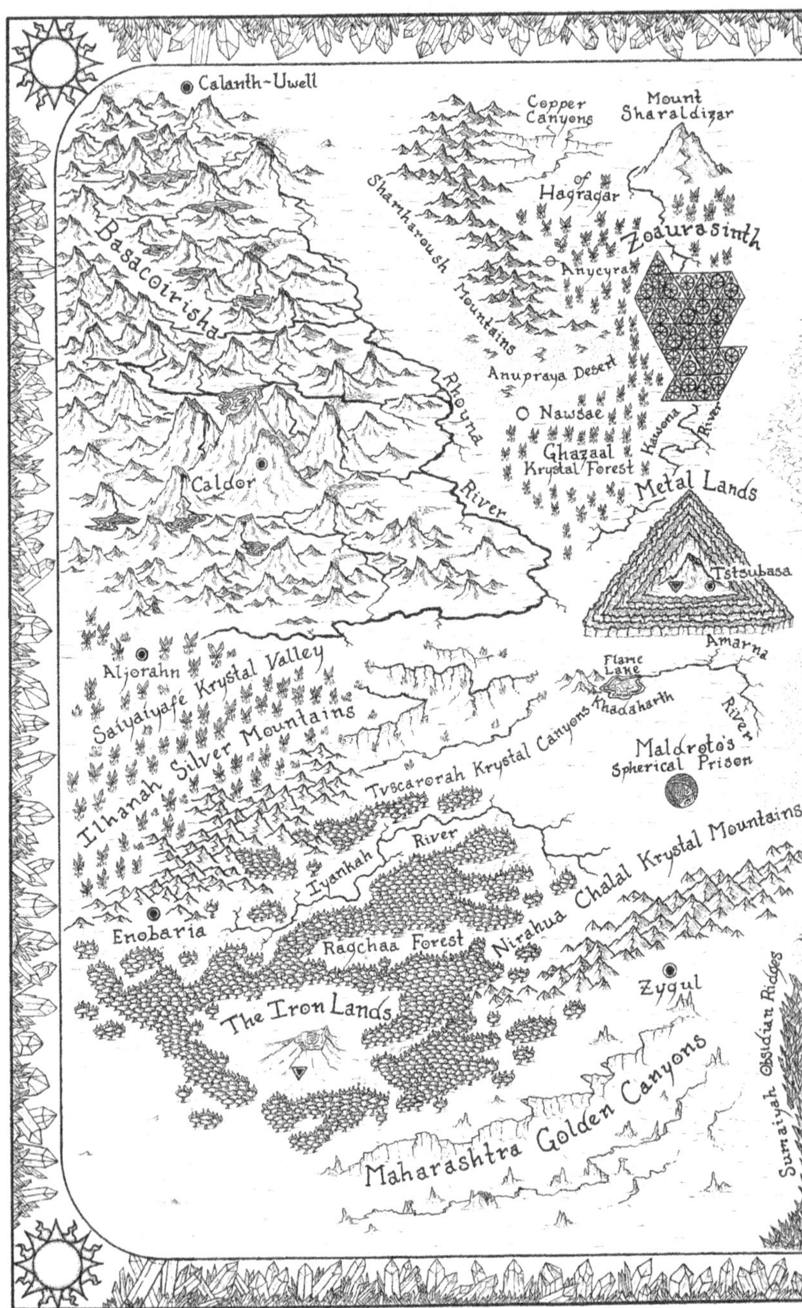
Calanth-Uwell
Copper Canyons
Mount Sharaldizar
Shamharoush Mountains
of Hagragar
Zoaurasinth
Anycyra
Basacoirisha
Anupraya Desert
Rhoyna River
Nawsae
Ghazaal Krystal Forest
Kawsona River
Caldor
Metal Lands
Tstsubasa
Amarna River
Aljorahn
Saiyaiyafe Krystal Valley
Flame Lake
Khadaharth
Ilhanah Silver Mountains
Tvscarorah Krystal Canyons
Maldroto's Spherical Prison
Iyankah River
Nirahua Chalal Krystal Mountains
Enobaria
Ragchaa Forest
Zygul
The Iron Lands
Maharashtra Golden Canyons
Sumaiyah Obsidian Ridges

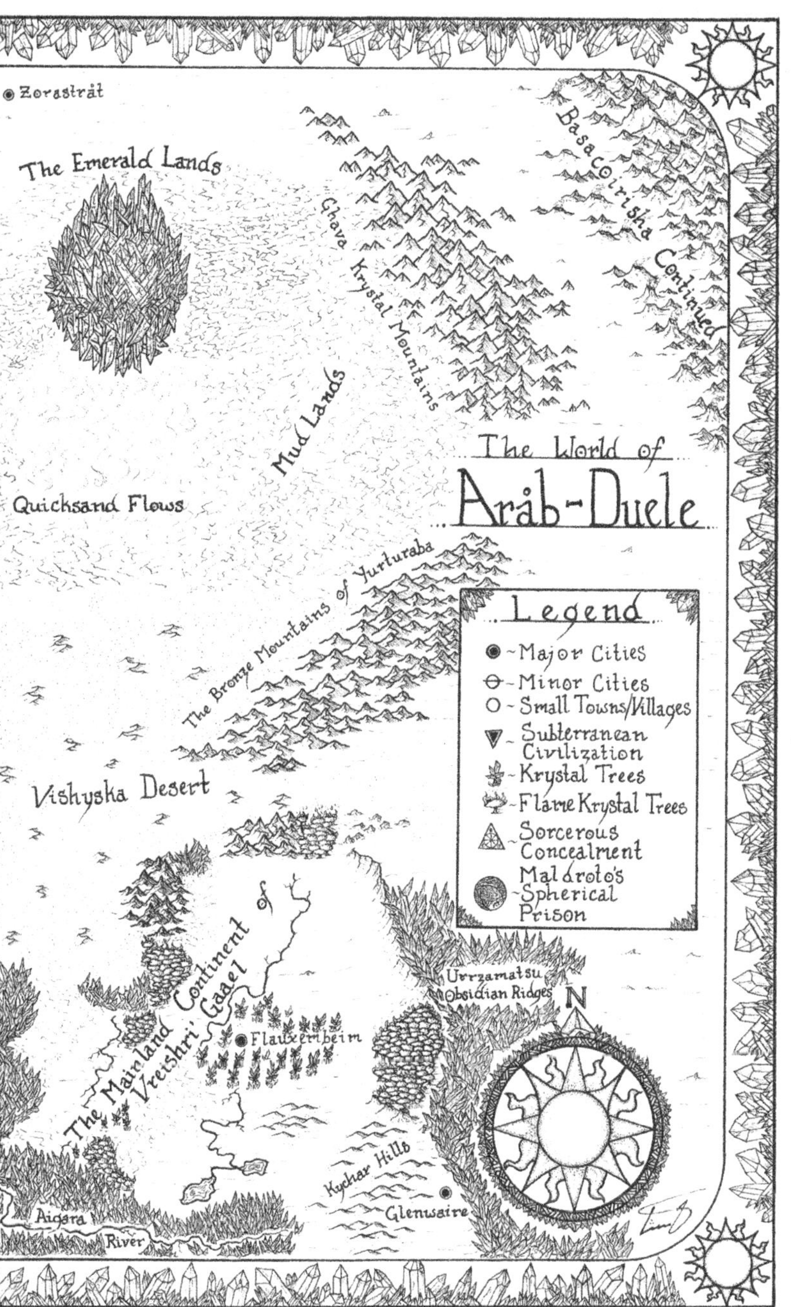

Zorastråt
The Emerald Lands
Ghava Krystal Mountains
Basacoirisha Continued
Mud Lands
Quicksand Flows
The World of
Aråb-Duele
The Bronze Mountains of Yurturaba
Legend
~Major Cities
~Minor Cities
~Small Towns/Villages
~Subterranean Civilization
~Krystal Trees
~Flame Krystal Trees
~Sorcerous Concealment
Maldroto's ~Spherical Prison
Vishyska Desert
The Mainland Continent of Vreishri' Gael
Urrzamatsu Obsidian Ridges
N
Flauxernbeim
Kychar Hills
Glenwaire
Aigsra River

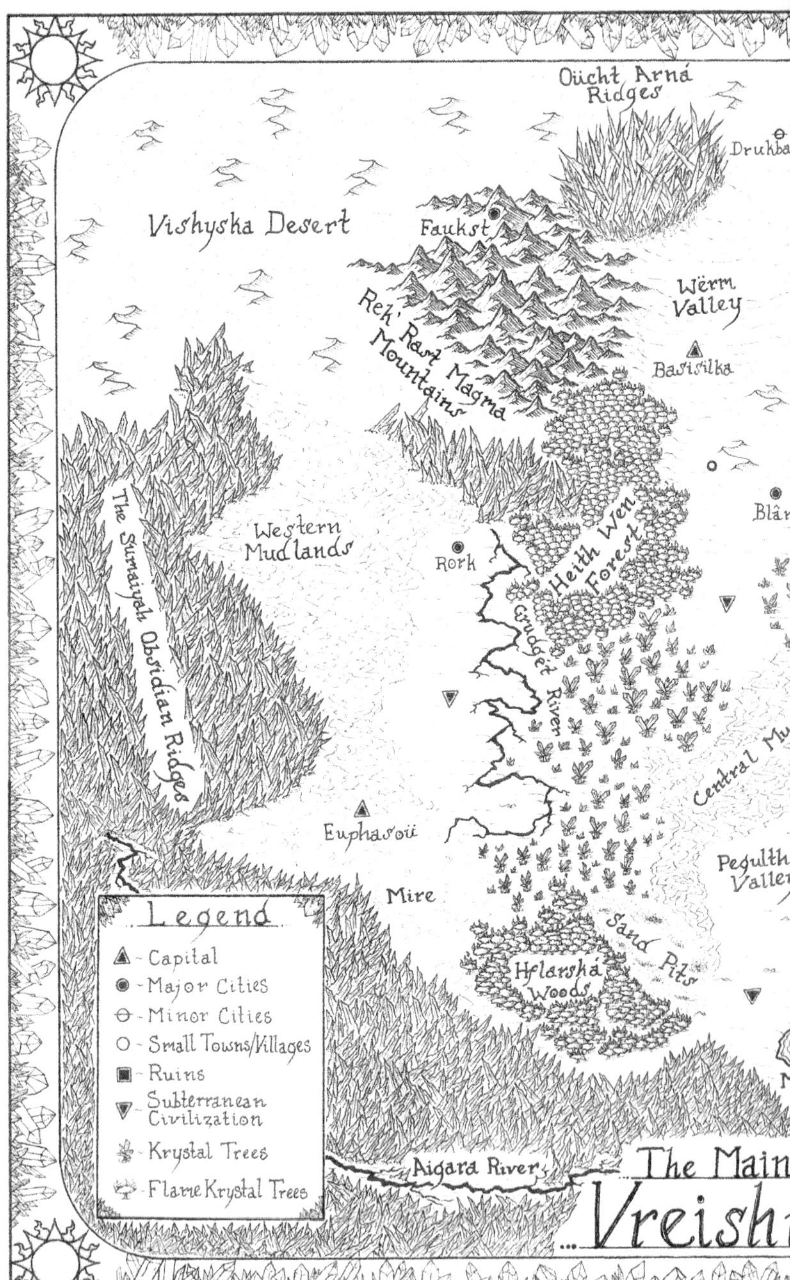
Oücht Arná Ridges
Drukba
Vishyska Desert
Faukst
Wërm Valley
Rek' Rast Magma Mountains
Basisilka
Blâr
The Sumaiyah Obsidian Ridges
Western Mudlands
Rork
Heith Wen Forest
Grudget River
Central Mu
Euphasoü
Pegulth Valley
Mire
Sand Pits
Hflarshá Woods
Legend
Capital
Major Cities
Minor Cities
Small Towns/Villages
Ruins
Subterranean Civilization
Krystal Trees
Flame Krystal Trees
Aigara River
The Main
Vreish

Drazok Forest
Orkgäust Rocks
k Ken Rancorn Mountains
Gnäst
Kuoffrapherel Cliffs
rn Fire Desert
Imperengú River
Exthanür Valley
Obsidian Lava Dwellings
Zukra Krystal Valley
Flauxembeim
Oen Dredgem Forest
Vicsh Snipe
Miesh Mik Sand Lands
Blue Asgari Hills
The Urrzamatsu Obsidian Ridges
Caves of Lagra
Magma Pits & Volcanoes
River
resk
Inch Bencht Flame Lake
Pools
Kychar Hills
N
Glenwaire
d Continent of
'Gaael

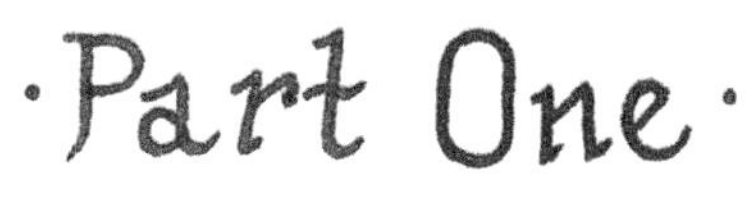
·Part One·
The Machinations of Fire

I

The Gravity Of Circumstance

The deck of the *Mantis* swayed unsteadily as the bane that served as the waves viciously bombarded the ship with aggressive, devastating force.

"She's sported another leak, Cap'n!" chimed the boatswain.

"Where's Jakowski?" barked Captain Pierce through the torrenting onslaught.

"O'm here!" Leonards Jakowski howled from the stern.

"I can't turn her away from this beast!"

"Suel!" bellowed the captain through foggy pillars of rain.

"I ain't seen him since she started!" wailed Swallows, the quartermaster, taking his captain's cry for a question.

"Jungabee! Go fetch third position navigator Drarris," signaled Pierce to his second mate.

"Aye, sir!" The small man leapt into the ropes and scampered away out of sight. White swords of lightning split the black veil of the sky. The *Mantis* rocked again with greater force than before, knocking most of the crew off their feet.

"We're gonna be torn apart by the rocks, sir!" roared Jakowski as he leaned the wheel precariously to the right, trying with all his power and capability to steer them all away from this cyclopean tempest of impending death.

"Where's Drarris?" cried the captain.

"Here, sir!" the third navigator confirmed with Jungabee at his right, his hand on Drarris's shirt sleeve.

"At your stations!" cried Captain Pierce.

"Stick your tails out between yer legs and suck your teeth into it. None of mercy or reprieve will be granted from such a monstrous, ailing bane!" Pierce shouted with gusto and a fervent, maddened delight.

Oppressive pillows of thunder burst in response and slashed and split open the sky. "Suel! God damn it, man! Why? Just why?!" Captain Pierce cursed himself.

With regret his stomach twisted and turned. *None of the other crew know. Only you do. It's because of you that he ain't here. You had to send him away, didn't ya. And for what?*

"Zammus Dre' Suel!" Captain Pierce wailed in anguish.

They weren't going to make it. Secondary and third navigators Drarris and Jakowski, both at the wheel, were trying to keep her at bay from the jagged teeth of the rocks which were beginning to close in around the *Mantis* and ensnare her in their grasp. The fangs of white rock dug and bit into the soft moist wooden flesh of the ship, viciously piercing it.

Splinters of numerous sizes and shapes bled from the *Mantis*, as rocks crunched, smashing and biting into her hull, slicing into the wood as easily as a spoon cleaves through runny egg yolk. Hopeless and breathing a poisonous nihilistic despair, her crew flung themselves into the rocks, leaping off the decks and into the spears of twisting rock, which eagerly embraced their bodies, immediately rendering them motionless as they broke and crunched, wrenched open. Those that hadn't jumped yet would soon be dead from the freezing water and drowning. The *Mantis*, devoid of her crew, had no choice but to yield to the demands of the elements and speed headlong into the rocks, crashing and splintering into shreds of wood. In the span of fifty-two seconds the one hundred and sixty foot-long, four-masted galleon had been shredded into irretrievable slivers.

Only one man of the keenest skills and sharpest of capabilities could have saved them all. Suel could have, in all possible truth. Yet where was Suel?

***

I was beyond disoriented, belly down floundering underwater surrounded by rapidly darting shadows. *Where am I? And where is here?* My thoughts slurred. *What is this? What . . . happened? . . . I don't . . . know . . .*

***

I, Zammus Dre' Suel, one of the most highly acclaimed marine navigators of Britain, was on a mission of appraised fortune, having been sent out by Captain Pierce with a pair of crewmates to lead an expedition on a series of isles. Rooted in these ocean regions was a common folkloric, legendary myth that had been circulating for who knows how long. Of course only the captain knew of its existence, as captains usually do regarding these affairs, right?

"On the Isles of Oriujange Drake you'll encounter the most valued of findings. Residing deep in the heart of that pile of dirt and rock you'll find values and treasures of the heartiest, most genuine dreams and holiest aspirations," Captain Pierce grinned imaginatively, blonde mustache whiskers twitching and twirling upwards with unrestrained glee and a mysterious endeavoring spirit.

"The noblest and grandest of embarkments, sir!" I had saluted, then inquired ambitiously, "Will this be a self-proclaimed or a teamed effort?"

"Send you on an assignment to a treasure island alone? So you can have it all to yourself and make a high praising title for yourself and leave us not a grain of absolute price? Are ya mad? What nonsense! Old man Parce and Deemetri will be accompanying ya. Take the longboat. Start preparations and charting course routes! Now, man!"

"Aye, Cap'n!" I confirmed.

Not long after Janitor Parce with his dusty white hair and the mottled freckled face of Deemetri, the cabin boy, were gently bobbing in the narrow frame of the *Mareissa* some meters below.

"I promise and swear I won't fail you, Cap'n."

"We've been on this ship for many a thousand and one days and nights and ya never 'ave. I know you won't now. Off ya go now, Suel. Be safe."

I nodded, "Always."

We clasped arms for a moment and separated. I descended into the longboat and raised my arm to the captain; he nodded and saluted in approval. The cabin boy in front of me and the janitor behind me began rowing and pumping the oars. Soon the *Mantis* was but just a speck on the monstrous settlement of the blue sea.

***

Three hours later as the ferociously bright bronze sphere of the sun was on the cusp of harboring on its travel west, the nose of the *Mareissa* plowed itself a home in a mound of moist orange sand.

"Docking!" I ordered, jumping off the side of the boat.

Parce and Deemetri followed and together we put our effort to beaching the longboat and camouflaging it in a leafy cover of palm fronds and making it safe from the grasping claws of thieves and marauders. Thunder melted in the distance, causing me to tilt my head to the sky in anticipation as I procured mental notes calculating wind speed and velocity, various air pressures and storm currents, numerous temperatures ranging from below freezing and sand-boiling, and lastly the degree of rain droplet impact.

"We make for shelter and to make camp in this tropical wilderness. You've secured your means of slumber?" I asked my mates.

"Aye, sir!" they obliged.

"Good." I myself double-checked my knapsack for linens, before replacing it back on my shoulders.

"Bring the boat."

"Sir?" the cabin boy remarked cautiously.

"A mother of monstrous, providential, baneful decree is to prey on the entirety of the Atlantic in two cycles," I proclaimed.

"What does that mean?" old pelican-haired Parce asked.

"I predict a hurricane in two hours," I said with blank unwavering accuracy.

"Let's go," I grabbed the stern of the *Mareissa* and turned her over. "Deemetri, help me."

We turned her belly up and walked under her, traveling up the hilly terrain of the island. *We've got two hours. One hundred plus twenty minutes. Seven thousand plus two hundred seconds,* ventured my mind.

***

Our camp location had been set up in a ravine deep in the inner brush of the island. Our place of rest was barren of trees, if there were any to double over in the case of the storm, which had thirty some minutes to strike and declare war on us. A deep tunneling cave presented itself to us, being almost nine meters high and five across. The *Mareissa* was laid down and we opened our canvas packs and procured linens. I unloaded my share of small cooking implements, these being worn wooden spoons, twisted copper forks, dull carver knives, and scratched, chipped tin bowls. Deemetri pulled out a small set of pans and fire stirring tools that Rogere, the ship's cook, had allowed us in tow to use on our expedition.

Parce procured meat grappling tools, made of both dull brass and wood alike. His set consisted of a variety of two-, three-, and four-pronged forks and pokers. We laid out our dinnerware. I instructed Parce to conduct a search for rocks to spawn a fire. He immediately began walking and bending about the floors of the cave in search for such morsels.

"I'm going to find us supper," I announced.

The cabin boy was observing the clouds and their variety of shapes.

"You know your duty as the ship's documentalist. Write down whatever scrap piece of information you find important and that you think may benefit us," I reminded him.

He produced a miniature notebook and pocketed quill, the latter being accompanied with an inkwell.

"Right," he said.

"Record. I'll be back with stock," I pronounced, leaving for the flower-dotted hills beyond. *Twenty plus six minutes until storm declaration and assault.*

"Moss that lines the walls of cave, possible protection from hard rocky head sleep on floor could offer cushion for head during resting. Cave mouth sports jagged edges, this may prevent against oncoming wind gusts from storm . . ." Deemetri scribbled down in his journal.

***

We had goat for dinner and three scrumptious bloated little lizards each around a meter and a half long. Parce quickly cooked them on sticks that Deemetri had found, while he and I dissected the goat into chunky strips and placed in sealed pots for our present supper and for the meals following tomorrow. While this ensued, Parce was stoking and feeding the flames. We supped shortly; the evening meal was decent craftsmanship. The sky above was as dark and vengeful as any abyss of hate forged for murder and annihilation. The three of us secured our linens and in cots of fabric wormed our way into their warm, nestled confines. We extinguished the fire out of safety and with the awareness that the wind would snuff it out regardless. Lightning struck overhead in the distance and the belly of the clouds split as water descended from their swollen bleeding flesh.

***

The storm was a serpent of infinite dark vile evils and morbidity. A draconic entity of no mercy or bounds of confinement. My companions and I had been spared the storm's brute, vigorous powers and strength, ever grateful to our homely sanctuary, the caves. The explicit damage was more than aggressively obvious.

"Holy mother Mary!" cried the elderly Parce.

Trees littered the ground, wedged, criss-crossed and shamrackled, helter-skelter in all which directions. Many rocks were smashed, cracked, and fractured as many of the large palms had assailed and crushed them.

"What of our boat?" asked Parce, bewildered and distressed.

My eyes darted around several times, scooping out and confirming the perimeter of destruction surrounding us. There was splintered bark, sand piled up in various mounds, and feathers scattered everywhere, but most bizarre were that were absolutely no bird carcasses to be found.

"We'll never salvage her in this wreck, Mason," I replied, looking into his old, withered face with both remorse and a measured grimness.

His face sunk, gray eyes only getting further and further from understanding his present reality.

"Pack your things. We have treasure to scout for," I announced, resolute.

The janitor's visage ripened automatically.

"Deemetri, we have to go," I said, nudging him awake. The cabin boy jumped to his feet and instantly took in his damaged surroundings.

"Father and son of Lord Will Shakespeare! T'was a most brutal and vulgar of tempests!" the young boy exclaimed.

I nodded. "Pack your bags. We have to explore and follow our mission as planned."

So many numerous preparations to go underway. What of the crew? Did they survive the storm? I fear the worst. How are we to know of their fates? The others cannot know or even suspect such an unfortunate travesty. Over burdening despair can give way to distrust and betrayal. They can't know, not yet. What of the crew? I fear the worst.

***

"Why are we here, Suel? What are we doing on this bloody wasted heap of an island? And what are you, as last I checked—as me and Deemetri are as ignorant as mice—searching for?" demanded old Mason Parce, holding none of his thoughts and implications back.

"We're lost. You're lost aren't ya? That's the fifth time we circled around that odd strange lookin' rock, and I know cus I stubbed me feet on it twice!" complained the cabin boy. I stopped and turned around annoyed and in disbelief.

"Look," I said, sitting down on a gray fragmented rock on my left. "Wish to know why we are currently on this rubble-strewn patch of dirt?"

Both figures were grim-faced and nodded solemnly.

"We are in this position due to Cap'n Pierce's orders. Supposedly by his claims this island and the isles around it are bloated with treasures and spectacles beyond our comprehension. He sent me to scout a mission and to survey the island to confirm his suspicions. You two are to help. If his claims are true, we can split up a reasonable amount of shares amidst ourselves and Pierce doesn't have to know the thought of it. You fellows must be rewarded for your assistance."

"Why not send the whole of the crew with his'self?" asked Deemetri.

"You were serious," old Parce whistled through a gap-toothed grin.

"Remember the storm, he could not have risked all of their lives on just a simple, possibly unpopular or indistinct rumor. If he had told them of these treasure islands and denied them entry via the storm, their greed and envy would have without a doubt outweighed their sense and logic and there would have occurred without a doubt a very violent and unavoidable mutiny."

"How did the captain expect us to confirm this treasure sanctuary of his if we don't know where the crew is and if they are even still alive, which is very unlikely?" Deemetri weighed their options.

"In all honesty, I dunno. And you're probably right. We've no boat and our only certainty is that the three of us are out for gold. And it could very well be just for us," I considered.

The tension and confusion noticeably dissolved and the three of us were off with a renewed sense of vigor, energy, and calm.

***

Towards the peak of day and after several unsuccessful circuits around this part of the island we were just as perturbed in our search and our desires continued to remain obscured and shielded from our sights.

"We've searched less than one fourth of this rock and we have no clues as to where we are supposed to even look," I groaned, frustrated.

We've been searching for hours! This is an impossible task. Suel, you fool! I cursed myself, despairing.

Sighing, I took a step and suddenly collapsed downwards.

"Sir Zammus!" croaked old man Parce.

I slid across a sleek surface at incomprehensible speed and just as rapidly stopped, the air blowing out of me as I thudded softly on my back. Bright lights gently glowed at the corners of my vision. *What just happened? Where am I? What's all that light? It's like an infinite glowing . . .* All around was subdued in a half darkness and the only noticeable light was an ominous iridescent fluctuation of luminescence in this unknown underworld.

"Sir!" my crewmates were crying from above.

"I'm alright, lads! Come take a look here! I think I found the golden jewels!" I shouted, grinning.

At the slight mention of gold and immeasurably vast aspirational treasures, Deemetri leapt into this dark world and shortly so did Parce; I caught him in my arms after he gently flew off the ramp. Currently our six eyes were contemplating the rainbow-colored glow of this elusive uncertainty. And so we began our flight and dash to the treasure of all dreams.

***

The amount was more than incalculable and insurmountable; it surpassed the most astute order of logic. Diamonds, sapphires, emeralds, rubies, glistening orbs of pearls and silver, flowers of quartz and towers upon glistening mountainous towers of gold.

"The crown of all crowned jeweled dynasties," sighed Janitor Parce in infinite pleasure as he sunk into a bed of gold, arms spread out, a smile planted on his wrinkled face.

"Bury me, lads," he brought a sheet of rubies and wonderful orange merriments to his neck.

"We're gods!" laughed Deemetri as he dove into a pool of diamonds, kicking and throwing jewels with his hands and feet.

I still couldn't fathom how much there was. "It would take a dozen *Mantises*—or several dozen for that matter— to clear out this cavern," I gasped, stupefied and shocked.

I looked around in total awe and was overwhelmed by various pleasures, my loins and heart set ablaze. Parce was sleeping and snoring softly in his golden bed and Deemetri was jumping and swimming into the ruby sapphire golden sea that we were more than waist-deep in. My eyes caught something to the right of me. I didn't really see it that well from the corner of my eyes, but gods be damned. I had to have it. Had to touch it. I made a launch for it, whatever the hell it was.

As I closed on it, I saw it was silver and sleek, warped into the carvings and configurations of a dragon, and beautifully studded with infused sapphires. Completely captivated and on the edge of salivating, I grabbed the charm.

And . . . it split into numerous silver tentacled sprouts and latched itself onto my chest, tightening and strapping itself on as an octopus engulfing its prey. Screams of horror and endless pain filled the cave as every aspect of my body was incomprehensibly pulled and stretched tautly apart and my sense of vision grew narrow, making everything seem smaller and higher at once.

"ZAMMUS!" old Parce and Deemetri shouted, their discordant cries ringing in my ears.

Purple flashed. Red flared. Yellow blazed and green light propelled me utterly blind into new, unknown surroundings. Water exploded all around me, crashing against me from all sides, encasing me. I couldn't breathe.

***

I was beyond cold and I felt myself thinning drastically and the space I was occupying was growing in both depth and volume. I was aware of three plaguing factors. *1. Heart and blood flow has rapidly increased to a rate that is highly dangerous and unsafe in persons. 2. There are numerous dark entities engulfing and closing in around me. I could die right here, right now. 3. Most bizarre, quite humorous and very odd indeed is the absolute lack of clothing that I possess. Why out of all reasons am I presently nude? No idea.*

As my head was spinning, processing my predicament and contemplating my next move, a large pole crashed into the water just above me and I was scooped up in what felt like a bristly basket composed of incredibly prickly sandpaper. It all happened so swiftly; one moment I had been paused in silent thought, disoriented in the cold water, and then in the blink of an eye, I was in this uncomfortable basket-net contraption that had the awful feel of porcupine and fresh cactus. The part nearest to my back was colder than frozen steel. From what my posterior could feel, it wasn't hollow like the sides of the *Mantis*, yet it wasn't blocky or frozen in place as metal either.

What was it then? The water surrounding me gushed and poured from the nest of thorns that clutched me, while bitter air clawed at me through the cracks of the wretched basket that I so wished to escape. Apparently, the basket had similar thoughts about me too, as it instantly opened up, spreading out and collapsing. As the walls holding me parted, I was simultaneously ejected from its bowl-shaped confines and roughly tumbled and slid on the ground, my nostrils scooping up orange-brown soil along the way. My long hair failed to protect my skull from bashing itself into a tree that had the reverberating hardness of stone. Then I heard a noise that didn't sound particularly animal. Before I could even ponder, another one of those tremulous, terrible noises pierced the air again. The ground was shaking and pulsing as if it had a beating heart of its own, and from what I could feel through this unsettling rapid shaking, the earth's heart was throbbing just as fast and full of fear as my own.

I dared to open my eyes, and in front of me, barely missing my nose were five yellow roots, each twice the girth of the old *Mantis*'s masts. Each of these gnarled, shriveled, bumpy tendrils had what appeared to be blocky obsidian ends that seemed in my eyes and opinion too wedge-like to be on a tree. My eyes kept glancing up, and all that I saw was continuous yellow bumpy bark that kept soaring ever upwards. My eyes scanned back down to those bizarre looking roots. I closed and opened my eyes. The roots wriggled and the black ends like sharpened hammers raked the ground and flung me forward into the air. With a surprised yelp I spun and landed poised on my feet. *It's time to get on the alert.* I grimaced, balling my hands into fists and curling my toes through the dirt.

What was this? Where was I? Why was I standing in a gathering of gargantuan trees that had black matter on their roots? And more importantly, where were my damn clothes?!

One of the trees moved and darted to the side, its dark roots dangling and pawing through the air. *What type of vegetation is that?!* My eyes darted around in circles.

More of the trees moved and I don't mean sway or leaned, I mean what I say: they got up, stayed in the air momentarily, then touched down again, replanting themselves. I looked up past the odd tree trunks and instead of seeing a canopy of some sort I instead wondered over a broad wall of mountain. Over this mountain, on the peak, was a taut, thickened cord, and resting on the tip was a pyramid-shaped face. It looked like some species of deranged, bewitched horse that was of a vast, immeasurable, and just incomprehensible size. This was easily the largest behemoth I had ever set eyes upon in my entire life.

I searched the space around me and made an estimate of ten ugly giant horse tree things. Suddenly in a flash, there in my back crept a pain so deep it was as though a spear of white fire had impaled me. Screaming, I collapsed on the ground writhing wildly and uncontrollably, suffocating as five thick yellow roots pressed me, melting me into the earth. I've no idea where the strength of will came from or how it entered my brain, but I couldn't stay down. Grunting with cyclopean strain, I heaved myself and, slithering from under its suffocating embrace, I was back on my feet again, only to be picked up by the roots that closed in around me once more and tossed me like hay to a sheep on the ground.

There it was again, the impossible burning savage pain in my back. *Fight it, Zammus!* I bit my lip, drawing blood as tears ran from my eyes. The other trees or horses were keeping their distance between me and this fat yellow brute. There was a gaping circle between the two of us. The roots swiped at me again, but I was ready for them. I hopped over the black ends and seized a grip on the bark, which to my surprise was full of canny handholds. Taking advantage, I scrambled up the trunk with hope for a moment or so before its other branch violently tore me off and I was on the ground once more, deposited with a sickening crunch that knocked out all my air.

I was swooped up once more like a child's toy, then released by those demonic roots and launched into the air. All of a sudden, gusts of wind were streaming over and darting around me in a crazy, ferocious gale. I felt the arrival of something blazing towards me. This tree trunk was unlike the others I had encountered; it was much thinner, very flexible and moved with motions like a whip. The trunk met my open arms and I latched on and felt about its roots, which to my shock were configured as spearheads of all sizes. *What is this magic and what sort of warped biological specimen was this? What was its making?* I wondered as I stuck to the branch and pulled on one of the infinite black protrusions. I wiggled a dagger-sized one in my hands back and forth, brutally applying pressure to both sides, while trying to keep my balance on this now-airborne monstrosity. The triangular-shaped object which, upon closer examination looked more like a crude knife, came free and sliced a large gash through my palm. Cursing and grimacing, I almost dropped it as thick slippery blood gushed from my hand, before switching it to my left.

The tree seemed to be bleeding as well from where I had torn free the makeshift blade. A purple fountain was flaring up in its place. An earsplitting wail pierced the air. With unbelievable force I was thrown off and flailed in the air, until I slammed into another trunk of the tree that was quite spherical. The bark served as needles which scratched up my chest and arms as I climbed higher up. I was in shock and astonished, at my inconceivable speed, reflexes, and profound sense of balance. My body was moving with near-perfect coordination before my mind even realized it. Gritting my teeth, I buried my weapon into its hide and quickly pulled it out and did it again. The tree-horse wailed in pain and trembled so violently that I lost my grip and fell off. It did a full reversal in the air and clawed its roots or black swords at me, slicing five long gashes across my chest.

My body trembled violently as I gasped, choking on my own blood. *You're not nearly done, Zammus. Don't even think about it,* my mind ordered. Reaching forward and wrenching sideways, I gripped onto those roots that could rip through flesh as my life depended on it. I drew my weapon and, placing my foot between a gap between roots, I drove my blade into the flesh that connected root to black mass. The beast beneath me tried its best to shake me off once more, but I used my blade as a sticker. I drove it deeper into the joint. I felt it sliding through what felt like muscle, then cartilage, and what I guess was bone, and finally, if possible, marrow. To my horror the black weapon slipped from my grasp, while purple fluid danced everywhere like a bright flame. I jumped through the purple sea as the shrieking screeched higher and higher, becoming more unbearable. *How can I still manage to hear anything at this point?* I groaned, gnashing my teeth together in pain and exhaustion as its wail of torment sliced the air to ribbons.

Purple blood splattered my wounds. Suddenly I was aware of my certain proximity to the ground. Sighing, I collapsed on the earth and began crawling like an infant searching around for the one thing that could save me, the long root that I had just severed. *Where the hell are you? Show yourself!* In a flash black blades dug into my left thigh and threw me into a pile of rocks; I howled as bones in my back crunched and cracked audibly. But I had to move, to live. With that thought I groped with my hand, hoping that the black root was here. For if not, then I, Zammus Dre' Suel, would be nothing but a memory and would die as a wasteful nothing in this demonic world of chaos where trees were murderers and mysterious savages. My spirits were more than rewarded as my right hand seized upon the black root. The tree beast came closer and I was quick to act. It swiped at me with one of its tree trunks, but I managed to roll under it to the best of my ability. Underneath it was like being in a forest. I could see all four of its broad yellow tree trunks.

I limped, my thigh practically split open and blood rushing down my leg, to the one nearest to me and thrust the sharp black object into its flesh. And as I withdrew the weapon, I must have sliced something major as the trunk went completely limp and sagged. Bits of purple gunk stuck to the spear-like object. I held the spear to my side and dragged myself over to where I assumed the tree's main trunk would be, the trunk with the pyramidal thing on top of it. The fiend surprised me then. The trunk that I had punctured swiped me out from under it, badly tearing my arm in the process. Barking out a cry of equal pain and strain, I was thrown into the trunk right in front of me, my body sagging and my spear soaring straight through flesh and hitting home to the bone with a resounding, definite thud.

Suddenly without warning, behemoth sails opened up and it began to climb against the resistance of the turrid air. Part of me just wanted to end this whole charade right now and let go of my lance and fall to the death. But another part of my mind was pushing me onwards. In a chaotic, disorganized wave fire exploded out of nowhere, walls of hot air pressing against me and forcing me to screw my eyes shut as I cringed, howling in fear. The rapid heat vanished just as quick as it came as the wind evaporated it, sucking and blowing it out of existence.

HUH?! FIRE?! My mind catapulted in terror.

WHERE did that come from? What is this? Fire! That changes everything! SHIT! I'm lost! I'm done here. My mind railed, horror paralyzing my muscles.

But what am I gonna do? Supposed to do? I guess die, right? Or! My thoughts viciously persisted, *I can use what's in my hand right now! Force an outcome! Or die. No regrets.*

Despite the overwhelming dominion of fear and lethal amounts of blood flowing freely from my flesh, resolution flowed through me as I launched the tool of my defense with an attitude of absolute determination into a bulge above that trunk that was becoming more and more identifiable as a limb. My enemy bellowed and bellowed away. Blood was running from my somewhat punctured eardrums. I too wailed in synchronized agony. I had to keep going, I could not give in to death so easily. I climbed over the shoulder and grabbed the spear. And, though the gusts of wind tried to knock me down into the abyss of darkness, I did not let go. I couldn't. There were many more roots on the beast's shoulder region. I did something then, digging and wrenching with my weapon I used the ebony spear to uproot another one of those sharp, long projectiles. The bane did not even react, or I thought it hadn't. Something from behind knocked into my entire side. It was the long flexible trunk with many sharp roots and it must have had the weight of an entire carriage.

My lungs heaved as I strained, multiple ribs cracking against the blow. I was thrown off the shoulders and would have fallen into nothingness had I not dug my two saviors into the main trunk of the devil. Its shrieks of pain were so disastrous, I honestly couldn't hear. Nothing and silence pervaded me as I entered the realm of absolute deafness, and all the warm purple fluid gushing into my ears didn't at all help either. Steam was hissing and rising from this pair of recent wounds. Both of my hands were horribly burned and my own bare red flesh and white knots of tendon were visible from my torn arm, but I couldn't release the objects embedded in its flesh, as that would be courting death. And that was not how I wished to leave this world.

I tightened my grip on the projectiles and, as if I were climbing a mountain, I stabbed and dug deeper into the monster's epidermis and maneuvered my way over to the juncture of trunk that met the triangular-shaped structure that seemed to direct this foul creature. Another trail of red heat exploded forward in discombobulated waves as fire was ejected forward. Mirroring the last time, it wasn't coordinated and didn't affect me despite the wind blowing the heat into my face and over my back. I closed my eyes as the torrent disappeared and the beast continued to roar.

I had lost so much blood and I was still ushering out lots; I wasn't at all steady on my feet and black dots were enclosing on the corners of my vision. Shaking, I collapsed on one knee at the base between two protruding roots. And screaming with my last ounces of strength I drilled the dark spikes through the nape of its neck and the beast shrieked loudly and dryly as the black blades pierced its vertebral column and split its spine from its head, which wobbled on severed nerve cables. In a spiraling spray of purple blood, the monstrosity and I fell together as one. I immediately lost my footing and its body rushed by in a canvas of skin engulfing me as I got caught rolling along its demesne, desperately scrambling to secure any random handhold. We sailed together and all that was heard through the air was the crispy shrill howling of the hot wind. My hands caught on something and I curled up inside some cushioned overarching root-like growths. When the body of my enemy hit the ground, every bone and fiber in my body gasped and cried out in infinite pain. But I was intact, cradled and protected in what appeared to be . . . claws?

I stared through the gaps of its yellow fingers that I had been thinking were roots. I looked at my foe in utter shock and disbelief. *The limbs were not trunks, but arms. There was no flexible trunk, but a tail covered in spines. The sails were obviously not sails, but membranes of a completely different sort. And the head was angular and covered in a crown of spines. How and why had I not seen this before? This is impossible! But clearly the evidence lies right before your eyes. Look around you.* This entire time, I had thought that I had been fighting a tree entity that was less horse than tree. I couldn't have been more wrong.

"I just killed a dragon."

I staggered and fell to the side and my head hit a rock. Everything went dark.

2

Mind Splits And Rifts, Just Break Apart

Something was breathing and squirming on my chest, some sort of mystical presence. It moaned, fluttered, and hummed while weighing me down. My breaths were labored and irregular. My muscles were as taut as chains. *My blood is freezing! Like the arctic!* My hand wandered over to my chest, attempting to claw at my wounds. *Where are they? How can this be?* I wondered sluggishly. *I was on the verge of death.* Warm metal tendrils engulfed my palm, enveloping my fingers, painlessly biting into my flesh, while rapidly crawling up my left arm. The metal growths flung themselves on my chest and began to constrict my torso. It was only then that I realized that I was bound. Long, thick heavy chains held my limbs. I gazed to-and-fro hoping to see where my bonds ended. They stretched out beyond my sight and trailed out into the corners of the darkness.

I was battered and overly puzzled and more than exhausted. *What had happened? To me? My mind? My mind ever since I had, had . . . what?* A waterfall of tumultuous memories rushed through me. Deemetri and Parce. The youth and his mottled face of innocence contrasted with old pelican-haired Parce with his gray wrinkly intricate spider-webbed visage, complex with faithful experience. *Where were they? How were they? Where was I? What was this existence?* I couldn't even fathom the events that I myself had wrestled through incomprehensibly. I have no idea how long I remained in that dark world, trapped in the protective, oppressive shield of my thoughts. My eyes closed shut as the colossal palm of fatigue closed in around me.

***

Harsh whispers of steel echoed and scraped the ground of my surroundings. Dark essences were entering my space, with steps that sounded like elephants treading on ice. *What wild beasts dare enter my domain?* I questioned as I stirred.

"Who goes there and what do you want?" I roared, frantic.

Growls and ferocious breathing filled the dark. Moments later a pair of glowing aqua eyes were illuminating the space. *We gotta escape! Now!* I was suddenly on my feet and clear of the chains that I had been in seconds ago, only now realizing that they were ten times my size and had not even been touching my skin. *How did I not realize that before? Was I that fatigued? Also, who and what were they made for?* A patch of golden light was floating somewhere to the right of me. My behemoth captor was slow and dull as a stone, probably unsure what to make of me; I easily slipped past them. I felt about for the walls, but there were none. Stone and shards of rock and other foreign objects bit into my calloused soles. The light was growing slowly as the air grew warmer. *Left, right, sharp turn, left again.* I didn't know where I was going; only that my muscles were pulsing and my knees and hamstrings flexing as I sprinted out of there. Stones crunched beneath my hard leather-like soles. *Where was I going?*

***

Shaken and feeling like a dunce, the beast growled and dug its talons into the dry, cracked dirt, mammoth nostrils flaring furiously in anger. It had been overly cautious, slow, and inattentive and had easily lost sight of its prisoner. However, the dragon's quarry wasn't far ahead. There was still time. The beast charged, galloping at full speed after the trail of confused footsteps.

***

I was rammed, hit by an unknown force as I was thrust forward. Claws tightened around me, the monster further securing its grip. Helpless as I was, I bobbed along accepting whatever was accorded to me. My prison cell served as the rough jagged enclosure of its paw. Its very texture felt of rusty daggers with blunt blades that didn't slice my flesh, but merely bruised it, particularly my ribs. I could feel the labored breathing of the gargantuan monstrosity resonating through its scales. Each step that the beast took was absorbed by my exhausted and utterly wracked body. Then I was blinded. *Light!* Infinite light incinerated my poor eye sockets. Shrinking back, I screwed my eyes shut. My eardrums exploded as sounds, growls, and roars burst forth, competing against each other, shoving themselves down my consciousness. My eyes slowly blinked open and I looked at the dark green and brown prison that contained me.

Before I could think to do anything, the claws released me and I was falling, tumbling through the air. I was violently slammed onto orange ground, my body crunching on impact. My senses revived themselves back to existence and my brown eyes zoomed in as they began to focus on everything around me. *An arena!* Large shadows were crawling and jumping. Blues, purples, reds, oranges, greens and yellows were seated in infinite rows. Soaring and leaping through the air above me, winged serpents hissed viciously. A large white blur descended from the sky, spread its wings, and released a shriek.

I jumped with fear. *What do I do? Am I supposed to kill yet another one of these foul beasts?* I took a very slow, deep lungful of sour, dragon-scented air.

"Come on and do something!" I challenged. The albino beast spat forth a gobbet of sapphire flame. I ducked and spun around and sprinted toward the center of the arena where there was a tall heap of chains. *Go investigate that! See if you can use it to your advantage!* I scrambled quickly. The demon was on my heels. An arm swiped me off the ground and I landed on the pile of chains that I was aiming for. *Nothing's broken?! How?* I delighted, though confused.

Who cares?! Does it matter? You're alive! Keep it up and more so keep your head in the game! Focus! Right!

I grasped one of the chains and swung it over my head. The links didn't go high enough. The dragon's purple eyes glowered in amusement. I swung the chain once more after I erected myself. The flying white mass swooped me up and I was dangling in its claws. *Perfect!* I looped one of the links over one of its yellow talons; it fit like a ring, and so the yanking began. I pulled as hard as I could, but it swiped its paw, trying to throw me off. I held steadfast as it tried throwing me around.

I tugged harder and the beast shrieked either in pain or in anger. I pulled harder with much more lethal force. *Splunk!* I felt a lesser mass detach from a greater. Purple liquid oozed from the wound and dripped onto the silver contraption strapped onto my chest. Then I was falling again and the claw that I plucked out fell onto the metal plate on my chest, the tip lightly tapping the center of the silver disk. The metal vibrated and a surging resonation echoed throughout my body and for the first time in my life as Zammus Dre' Suel, my body was not my own or under my absolute control. My limbs were jerking with a will of their own, twitching uncontrollably. The flesh that served as my skin ballooned out enormously as muscle swelled beyond comprehension.

"What's er ppening t e?" I choked out through swollen lips as deposits of fatty tissue swallowed my face and my sinuses closed up. *What's this? HH . . . h . . . air? AIR?!* Unimaginable pain crept out of my tailbone and quickly escalated up my spine, violently peaking in my wide almond-colored shoulder blades, which began to split and rip through genetic elongation. My back muscles arched as did my entire spine. My arms and legs severely folded in on themselves, while silver bones began climbing out of my skin. All the more the fibers that held me together were slicing themselves apart. I collapsed on the ground, inexplicably burrowing several meters through the earth. The prehistoric part of my brain, the oldest aspect of me, the most ancient vestige that monitors life survival instincts twitched, now fully activated. The reptilian part of my mind was chiseled, sharper than it had ever been. The white dragon decided to investigate and stick its obese snout down in the crater that I had made.

I struck out and sliced six gashes across the right side of its face. I shot out of my pit, ramming my talons up its abdomen and out of its back. Flapping my wings harder with my forearm still in its torso, I tossed the dragon's body up and batted its head clean off with a swipe of my claws. Incredulous, I watched both descend below and plop to the ground with a crunching thud. I roared, feeling immensely confident and enjoying the sensation of this newfound power. Four dragons from each of the four corners of the arena flew forth to challenge me, all armed with chains. The audience of dragons roared in excellent approval. I bared my fangs in great excitement, roaring as well. Anticipation was pounding through my new, enriched muscles.

To my right lay a brown brute, while speeding towards me were two fellows: one orange and the other a dark shade of azure. Above me a great, monstrous purple blur was suspended. I closed my eyes in anticipation. A grenade of pain detonated in my shoulder and the entirety of my right side as kilotons of force slammed me, generated by the hulking masses of the beasts which had rammed their brown and blue shoulders into mine. The sharp hissing sound of weapons caught my eye. Heavy loops swarmed over my left arm, while a hook pierced my hide. I roared savagely, furiously working my jaws as I bellowed in immense pain. The chains securing me suspended me taut in midair. Pain was firing and bursting from the hooks that had impaled my side. Something huge penetrated my vision and slammed into my face. Before I could react a thick orange coiled slab which had to have been the size of a blue whale, pummeled my face and neck from the other side. Blood burst through my mouth and nose and some of my teeth shattered like shrapnel as they crunched and punctured the roof of my mouth and tongue. My brain was on fire. *I'm feeling severely compromised skeletal structure and torn, shredded muscles!* The itching and nuisance that were the hook and chains that had sheared and torn my flesh faded out from my awareness as my body sunk downward through the air.

The shadowy curtain of the great purple monstrosity dove down from its corner of the sky, blazing towards me at unbelievably frightening and impossible speed. My body bent and collapsed inwards, my spine snapping and limbs thrashing and shuddering in convulsions as the improbable strength of the purple dragon's bulk collided with me. Bright colors and dark shadows burst across my vision and I saw stars. My mind fragmented in an eruption of rainbow-colored light.

***

I didn't know where I was. There was a dry, barren landscape. A hot wind blew past and my stomach growled. There was a pain in my back. Something was underneath me. A rock? The pebble underneath my spine jumped in a way that a mere rock never could. I jerked my body to the left in discomfort and got off the damn thing. The ground blew up dust particles as a brown hare leapt past me. The obsidian sphere that had been beneath me quivered with a life of its own. As cracks were adorning it and molten flames raged from within, the stone dissipated in all directions, incinerating every aspect of the barren landscape.

***

Dust spewed all around me as my shoulders erupted from the sand that had buried me. *Where am I? And how did I get here? Wasn't I in that weird arena? What's going on?* I was covered in dried patchy smears of purple blood. *That's two dragons I've killed in this hellish waste,* I thought bitterly. I couldn't help but feel that something imperceptible was watching me. Sand burst, exploding in my face and sending me spinning through the air, as something leapt upwards from underneath me. As I rolled through the air a long pink tongue reached out and like a rope latched itself onto my ankle and threw me down onto the ground. *What in the hell is happening?!* I panicked. Whatever this thing was, it had ten legs and these latched onto me, each of its ten flat paws ablaze and engulfed in flashes of fire that were burning my skin.

"Aghhhhhh!! Get off!" I howled in pain, trying to grab a hold of the creature and force it off of me. One of its ten feet pressed down on the silver plating on my chest. Immediately the steel lightly hummed and depressed and the creature pulled back. The process of swelling and skin splitting began once more.

After red and golden reptilian tissue had emerged, violently shattering my frame, the protrusion of angular wings burst from my spinal column and as before, like a pufferfish my proportions drastically enlarged in cell and bone mass. I breathed through a pair of improved nasal cavities and my overly wide shoulders rolled, feeling tighter and leaner and much more capable. I glared down at the ten-limbed scoundrel who, having more than it expected, was recoiling and running off, its flame-filled feet leaving scorched patches in the sand. *Enough blood has been spilled. I need to think and most of all get my bearings.* Dirt billowed in a cloud as my wings sliced the air and I took off in search of a sanctuary that could birth a clean shower for my thoughts.

Not less than five minutes later all the fatigue and exhaustion finally caught up to me like an inevitable, unstoppable tidal wave. Just like a carriage collapsing after many years of relentless wear and tear, breaking down all of a sudden when out on the road, likewise my wings retracted out of existence and everything dragon about me shrunk and disappeared.

"Aghhh! No! NO! I swear, come back!" I screamed in horror.

I continued to shrink all the more until all that I was, a naked man, remained. Brown murkiness dwelt below. *The distance and height from the approaching ground is unknown, latitudes and longitudes are a mystery. Enter impact position!* Screaming, my voice raw, hoarse and cracking I braced myself, tucking my knees into my chest. *You've defied death long enough, you won't escape! You can't!* All this while I had been frantically slamming the plate on my chest, which like the stubbornest of lovers refused to be stimulated by my touch. *Accept your fate, Zammus.* I resigned myself. The infinite broad milky striations of the tobacco-colored mire were approaching closer and closer to my soon-to-be obliterated existence. The kilometers had now zipped down to mere meters from impact.

"Death, I offer you my open hand," I breathed, fully acknowledging the facts of the situation.

Feet from impact. My face grimaced into a wicked contortion of skin and forced wrinkles. Inches from impact. *Suel, you fool!* Mud! It shot up my nose, raced through the portals of my ears, and the highway of my mouth and throat. I was beyond the mere state of jumbled discombobulation. Mud. There I lay breathing in nothing, but the muddiness of the situation. Mud was all I knew . . . all I knew . . . knew.

***

All concepts of time were lost. How long did I stay unconsciously immersed within the muck? Knowing nothing but muck? I've no idea. I awoke having no sense of anything or clarity. *When was the last time you had something to eat?*

"I don't know," I rasped.

Wunk! Something flashed overhead. My head sunk and my eyes rolled back in my head.

3

Beyond Mere Contingencies

Heat shone through the doors of my eyelids and I leapt out of my unconscious state. Faintly I made out a pair of small lights. And closer still, the rays of an ever-flickering green flame which was seated on a bed of green coals. I sat up and quickly grew dismayed and then alarmed to find my limbs secured by what felt like vines which were composed of thorns and filed bones. Parts of my skin were damp where the thorns had punctured it. *I'm alive?! I'm alive! Where am I? And who's that?! Didn't I fall from the sky?!* My mind was firing off thoughts like bullets. *Enough of just being and reacting! Damn it, Zammus! Get it together!*

"Show yourself, you coward! Why am I tied up?!" I barked.

The eyes said not a word.

"Say something, you fool!" I raged, attempting to burst out of my restraints, which only resulted in my skin being pierced all the more. The figure, which was distinctly male, stood up and I sized him up to be about my size. His torso was bare, improbably muscled, and he wore dirty form-fitting and soiled trousers. His feet were bare and ended in claws. He growled and, eyeing me steadily, picked up something long and leapt over to me, clearing the flames in a single bound and bringing his weapon down. I rolled over, missing the blow. He swiped at me again and missed slicing my right arm, but not the ties securing it. He came yet again and I spun about. The bonds holding my left arm split and fell to the ground. My enemy swung his blade once more and would have sliced off my elbow had I not jumped to the side and swung at his ribs. My skin split as it rubbed against scales. The foe grunted lightly and drove his fist into my abdomen.

I collapsed onto my knees, choking on the combined solution of saliva and blood. *My intestines have been shoved up my throat, plucked out of my midsection, and dragged out of my buttocks!* Ragged coughs raked me and I lay spitting up my innards on that dried patch of mud.

"What are you waiting for?" I hissed, seething as blood trailed from my mouth. "Come on, do it already! Damn it!"

The aggressor came over to me and, snarling, grabbed a load of the locks that were my hair. Holding me by the head, he raised his blade. My eyes screwed themselves shut.

"Do it!" I screamed.

The blade raced through the air. *Dunt!* The edge of the blade lay buried in the ground. *I'm still here! Alive!*

"Why?" I asked.

What did he cut? Raising my detached bundle of hair, he hovered it in front of my face momentarily and then offered it to the ravenous emerald flames. He then walked around the now blazing fire and disappeared into the dark civilization that was the mire.

"Hey!" I called after him.

For an awful and sinister illimitable pool of dreadful time my mind dwelt in the dark shadows of the situation that I was floating in. Within the caves of my mind an analyzing monologue was ensuing.

Within the monsters of our universe of solar grasslands inhabited by the multitudes of vast species of elephant ascendance, which through the unknown copulation of time and many of his ungulates, I, Zammus, can't help but feel lost in this wild multiverse of realms delving from the vortex of selfhood to the ghouls that lay scattered on a level of consistency that not even the youthful dust speck could fathom to understand in all of his Herculean stature of scavenged deceased life minuscules. Am I just a scattered gathering of pointless space matter not unlike my dust ball brethren?

"Who could say?" I answered.

The owner of the fire returned, arms laden with bundles, one of which was deposited at my feet and revealed itself to be a punctured plant tuber that had the bizarre shape and size of a rabbit. Without thinking of the digestive consequences, I sunk my teeth into the plant-flesh and with two rough hands massacred the damn thing with the ferocity of sharks slaughtering the bodies of dead whales. The moment that the first bites entered my stomach glowing red trails of light began crisscrossing my skin. The figure across stared, not comprehending as the torso of the creature in front of him began flaring up. As this progressed the oozing and dripping patches of my skin were born anew as the sacred and most ancient spirits of the flame worked within.

Whatever phenomenon was occurring, it felt miraculous; I could feel the universe, its creators, and all of its inhabitants flowing through these veins. *Oh, the surge!* Movement whizzed, stirring the dust and billowing up in red clouds of dirt from meters behind the figure in front of me. Whatever was approaching, the dry mud under our feet was cracking and splitting rapidly. Leaping to my feet, I was ready to desert him in full honesty. *But he hadn't taken my life when it had been so easily in his hands. Why? Then he brought me food when I was on the brink of starvation. Why again?* My mind circled endlessly.

The vibrations in the ground were making the blood in my head and ears pulse and causing the forms scattered around the fire to jump. Rocks and muck exploded into fountains and skyrocketed into the air as the ground split. Then I was airborne? Falling or flying whichever it was, my eyes were fixed on the orange glowing tendrils that were slithering from the expanding molten, hissing orifice in the dirt. I cried out as I slammed back hard onto the ground, falling on my right hip. Growling at me either in warning or fear–I was not sure–the figure leaped over to me and extended his scaly palm. Although it felt of rough jagged stone, I allowed him to pull me up. I watched frozen in place as he moved his palm in a jerking, rapid motion, his fingers facing the ground, the flat surface of the dirt ascended into a mountain and lengthened itself into a rod of hardened sand which the fellow grabbed as the tip trisected into the prongs of a trident. *What just occurred before my very eyes?* I gasped.

The ground detonated as three fiery cylinders erected themselves. I immediately felt the heat slithering towards me on dozens of sharp pointy appendages that were incinerating the ground. Layers of flame engulfed the enormous body of this demonic beast. *Must be over one hundred plus meters long!* I marveled. Staring up at it, I was beyond stupefied. Looking down, it regarded me, its red-black eyes glistening, its head was as large as the entire *Mantis* had been. I was still as a statue as its colossal snapping mouth parts divided and the white molten core of its throat revealed itself. Before I could do anything, the behemoth dove down and, with its mandibles spread wide apart, swallowed me whole.

From within the hot moist confines of its jaws I refused to accept my fate.

"I love you," I mumbled with a strange feeling I didn't understand, utterly unsure who or what I was addressing. As my hand drifted, touching my chest, I felt not flesh but the steel of the plate. *Everything came down to this!* Pounding all my force into the disk, I howled as the body I possessed warped out of itself. The beast's head burst open and exploded as my body transformed in an outrageous eruption of muscle. The beast that swallowed me burst into molten flesh as my wings furled open on either side of me, hurling black gore and viscera everywhere. Swallowing hot, putrid air, I observed the fellow below me and the two remaining monstrosities slithering rapidly. Descending at full speed I grabbed one of the wretched slugs in my jaws and as I writhed and shrieked, I dug my front claws into it and spreading them further into its innards I ripped it apart. Black blood exploded, splattering all over my face and chest. Not far off my companion was still wrestling with his own beast.

Propelling himself in the air from four sand steps that he just made, he ran up and jumped off. With his trident raised I watched him dive towards the beast's abdomen. Foreseeing its death, it turned its mammoth head and buried its fangs into his side. He cried out and with the last ounces of his strength he allowed the weapon to hover in the air and with some force or another propelled the trident through and out of the beast, which immediately released him. As he fell his weapon disintegrated into the air. Flying over, my wings swooped down and I gently caught him in the left pad of my front foreleg.

"Who and what are you that latches onto me? Release me, foul dragon!" the lizard man yelled.

He speaks! My mind observed, completely shocked.

"You talk!" I growled, overtaken with surprise.

"What doesn't! Where's that unusual character who accompanied me at the start of this battle?" Blood oozed from his body.

"Listen to me, you're losing a lot of blood. What's the nearest civilization around here?"

"Euphasoü," he said, pointing left and forward.

"How long will that take?"

"We'll be there by noon," he wheezed, "The venom will burn through my veins and race through my heart in six hours."

I flapped my wings faster.

"How do I know that you're not a malignant beast who isn't carrying me to my death?" groaned the lizard.

"Well, first off, you almost killed me–when I was smaller, that is–and you brought me food, helped me up, and for the strangest reasons you cut my hair!" I explained.

"Though confused, those did all happen by my hand. How are you as you are?"

"I myself don't even know," I said, being honest.

Should I even trust him? Can I? He saved me and clearly has helped.

"I'll tell you only if you promise to tell me yours," I spoke.

"Sure, it's the least I can do after all this," he said, gripping one of my claws.

"Very well," and so I began. The confused twine of my tale began with the introduction of the *Mantis* and her crew and then descended into confusion as a land of giant lizards came into play. This was when the injured fellow spoke, "So that jewel you were mesmerized by, from what you're telling me, it took you here and it's on your chest?"

"Indeed."

"Ahh, hmm. True to my word, I'll narrate the woes that have befallen me," my companion huffed.

Bestowing even more of his trust in my hands, he related who he was and how fate had deprived him of affection. Born with the name of Dar Vagoue, he had been the first of four and was raised in the emerald forest of Heith Wen. His parents had fallen ill by an unknown sickness which had quickly seized the throats of his siblings. Not soon after, all but him lay in the clutches of the dark. In the arms of desperation, being bereft of his senses and seized by madness, he snuck into the neighboring city of Rork in the quest for herbs.

"For a day and night I wandered and searched until, by the dawn of the third day, after so much laboring it revealed itself. The moss of hetatch, a well-known remedy! Placing as much as possible in the confines of my knapsack, I was unaware at the time, for the most part, of the vipers on my heels. Now that I think of it, there were times when I heard a rustling, but the cover of night hid them well as the cowards that they are. Back in Heith Wen, I administered the edible moss to my family and with feelings of devout fidelity swelling in my chest I went to take my repose in the form of sleep.

"Awoken by the signs of activity, my heart thrummed with joy which evaporated instantly as my eyes perceived the destruction that lay in my midst. The punctured throats of my family members and coiled tails slithering out of sight. Screaming in rage and sorrow I was silenced by an unknown force. I woke with a head throbbing in pain and I was conf–"

"Go on, my friend," I gently urged. Looking down at his curled-up form, my eyes beheld him in a bed of hardened orange fluid, which had glued my claws. My wings hastened to get Dar to Euphasoü alive.

***

Endless sand dunes with randomly scattered patches of reflective green rock finally loomed beneath me as the structures of a city came into view. Pillars of stone along with innumerable huts dotted the ground. I knew not where I was or who or what to go to. *Lost and Dar is dying! Damn it, Zammus!* I cursed. Dragons were milling about to-and-fro in the dozens, navigating and maneuvering through shops and merchant stalls and crossing busy thoroughfares. Placing Dar's form beside a green iridescent outcropping of stone, I spread my wings and breathed as I stretched out my left talons which were suffused in hardened orange blood.

Howling away through the air, a specter or a ray of light whirled by and in a blast of hot air I was knocked off my legs.

"Dar?"

Dar wasn't there. He had vanished. The ball of energy collided into a mountain ridge and in two exhausted claps of air I was in pursuit. Clumsy, lacking strength, and with mental determination that was extinguishing, my eyes and other senses glazed over.

***

Witnessing her pursuer stopping as if he had hit a wall, she observed, absolutely captivated as his body began to shrink and fold in on itself. Squinting, she swirled over to him and back in the cave she gleamed at her two prizes.

***

Pillars of leaves filled my vision as green bursts of sunlight. Yet there was no sun, which confuddled me. Trees pounded the soft mud in detonations that mirrored cannon fire. Whatever gargantuan creature was wreaking forest havoc was going to crush me to ribbons of flesh unless I fled its path. An earthquake gushed behind me as I felt three trees hit the ground which tore open into cracks of instability beneath my feet. Turning my head back to witness the architect of such grand demolition, my eyes perceived a scaly, robust predator with all sorts of tusks and horny protuberances jutting about its red, gold, and copper features.

Stark golden-yellow eyes ten times the size of a mule cart regarded me. Death was pursuing me himself. I was beyond petrifaction. A silver whip that ended in four prongs crept out of the unseen mouth of the villain.

"Run," the tongue leapt.

Stupefied beyond comprehension, I lay motionless.

"RUN!" thundered the voice, causing my whole

body to move slightly and tremble in sweat and the trees to dance in the gale.

The gods themselves were here to persecute me! Again! I took off in a blur and, looking back, I perceived a brute five times the size of a galleon. I was knocked into the ground as wings the size of churches furled open. Bowing in submission, I allowed rows of teeth to consume me. No swallowing took place; the lower jaw hung open, but the slightest attempt to escape would result in my impaling. With no choice I watched through the gap of the jaws as grass and greenery passed by in rushes. Dead rotting matter and flesh overwhelmed my nostrils and mouth. The bright red-orange crater of a volcano loomed ahead. The beast leapt with great agility and enthusiasm into the molten basin. Lava flooded down its maw to engulf me.

4

An Annoying, Accelerating Madness

Covered in oceans of sweat I leapt awake to experience feeling the disk on my chest raging with intense heat as it bled red with molten intensity. Howling in pain beyond comprehension my body began to convulse into transformations that weren't like the previous conditions. The envelope that was my skin swelled and crumpled out of itself as the cells and muscles that were reproducing beneath shoved themselves out of my flesh in glowing crimson globules. My chest was horrifically splitting in two, my sternum savagely bisecting as the plate began to shift. My body rose, lengthening and erecting itself into a wobbly pillar as it wrenched and twisted, spasming in convulsions. With an air of finality my warped and fractured body collapsed into a pile of red burnt scales.

***

Yvylara, the dragon who had taken Zammus and Dar Vagoue captive, had witnessed this frightening spectacle. She blew fire onto the heap the small unknown creature had been reduced to. With an air of indignation she whipped her tail, sweeping off the remains, which were driven off the cave ledge and carried downwards by the wind. Orange casing cracked as Dar Vagoue began to choke on the poison that had been administered by the magma centipede five hours and forty-six minutes prior, causing her to turn her head in alarm at he who had been so silent and unconscious. Her concern peaked as his convulsions intensified. Grabbing him with one of her hind legs she disappeared in a trail of white and brown. Reappearing, she found herself on the edge of the Hflarská Woods and also in the domain of her brother.

***

I was falling and looking down or up, yet whichever direction I looked, I saw nothing but endless red loops. *Whoa! Where am I? What happened back there? Where's my body?! Do I have one?* My thoughts were racing as I looked all around and saw nothing but air, no flesh, no nothing. Opening my senses even more, if I could call it that, I expanded my awareness and was totally confused at witnessing a tangerine-colored path looming directly before me. *Just a moment ago this road was miles beneath me and now I can dip my face into it. Huh. I'd like to,* I thought placidly. The molten tomato-colored surface parted and rippled as my essence reached into it.

***

Liquid bled from above in a multitude of values. My form was being bombarded by bullets of color from the brightest positive to the darkest negative. *Hey, I have a body again!* I rejoiced. A countless squadron of droplets struck me simultaneously in my broad back, my chest, the crown of my head, and my sides in the forms of pinks, greens, yellows, purples, blues and oranges. To my vast horror each glob of paint that hit me left a pebble-sized hole of emptiness, a void where there was no flesh, no blood, just nothing. *My body is disappearing!* A chunk of gray the size of a grapefruit bombarded me.

"Agghhhh!"

This negative matter forced itself like a parasite beneath the wall of my forehead and slowly gnawed its way through my brain. I sunk onto one knee as I collapsed from a lime-colored sphere that had dissolved my other knee cap. My teeth ground together as my face twisted in a grimace.

"Aughr!" I cried as pink clumps just passed through where my intestines had been.

"A splendid day, don't you agree, Zammus?" The red and golden dragon lay undetectable in a sea of orange plants.

My mouth gawked open at the spectacle, as a yellow orb swallowed my nose, staring at the enormous monster that lay seated some paces away.

"Well, stop your ridiculous gaping or you'll lose your whole mouth, eyes, or both!" spat the reptile placidly.

"Help me . . . pl . . . " stretched my tongue.

Crossing his eyes in amusement, a scratchy sound resonated from his throat, causing his four-pronged tongue to slap the air.

"What a most ludicrous suggestion! If I did, I'd lose my entertainment," chuckled the dragon.

A lavender missile tore through the side of my head and three things happened. My left eye ceased being and shortly after my right. Collapsing on my stomach and howling in desolation I was hit through the spine and my heart stopped beating as it was evaporated into nothingness.

***

Dagger tips! Were all pressing into my body! I pushed myself painfully from the wedge-shaped rocks below me. They resembled gray arrow tips.

"Wait, you just saw gray!" Looking around with a stupid gargantuan grin, I took in the black mountain above me that was belching out red breath, the yellow sands beneath me, and the bright orange streams around me. "Eyes!"

I can see! See! My sight! Happily rubbing my eyelids, I laughed like a buffoon, launching my mirth all around.

"Good for you, how fortunate that you can use those useless eyes of yours," scorned a voice from below. "They're still no use if you can't be aware of me unless I speak."

A golden eye that had to be as wide as a mast is tall smirked at me from under the rocks that held me. In an eruption of rock fragments and orange flames, I was airborne as the dragon unearthed himself. Settling on rocks that could have been the ground or his back I trembled and bristled at the same time, not forgetting his lack of help in my previous moment of dire need. We rose into the air as he unfurled his massive wings. There was a brief pulse of light and then I was looking into the maw of the volcano that I had spotted not five moments ago. *Or was this a different volcano? How?* Before I could open my mouth to voice my thoughts, the grand beast bearing me veered to the left, twisted very abruptly, and lost its passenger.

All I could do was scream and corkscrew in the air as I descended into the mountain's molten jaws.

***

His eyes were closed and rimmed with deep emerald and bright, reflective red copper-colored eyelids.

"You're a deeply pathetic creature."

Green wisps of mist clung to the air, thick and languorous as smoke and hanging low to the ground in fat, hazy clouds. Soft diamond-colored growths caressed my stomach, thighs, and face, which angrily contorted and twisted into blossoming rage.

"HglephchrRRR!" I spat, launching myself and spinning onto my back. I found startlingly stark golden eyes peering down and a bright red copper angular snout that was a yard above my head. Black lips folded and divided to reveal inviting brown-silver teeth, each appearing to be longer than my height. Squeaking in fear I stopped myself. *Enough running! Face this beast! Take control, Zammus.*

"Yes, be in control, you dolt," I whispered.

The demonic beast cocked its head quizzically and its eyes twinkled in amusement. Blinking and breathing evenly as my heart spun in my chest, I demanded, "Where am I? Where are we? What is this?"

A silver tongue that ended in four tips that had to be at least two meters long spun backwards into the air as the dragon lazily spread its mammoth jaws, yawning. Regarding me with a blank expression, he closed his eyes.

"Where are we? Where am I? Tell me!"

Turning his jaws in my direction, his tongue flicked out of his maw and like a tentacle wrapped itself around my waist!

Wings the size of a cathedral shattered my eardrums as they massacred the air beneath them. The diamond forest was naught but a speck below. I couldn't breathe! Gasping weakly, I dangled helplessly, the strength to fight this being vanishing. It was hopeless. The air vibrated as a tremor shuddered through the scales of my captor. His entire body throbbed and pulsed violently. My teeth were chattering like stones, eyelids fluttering, skin creasing, and every tendril of hair shaking and dancing. Golden skies embraced by a purple sun gazed down openly at a translucent ground below. Half a heartbeat later obsidian-colored rock fangs roared up miles away. Dead, desiccated brown rocky earth embraced us. Descending, his hind legs met the cracked sable rocks softly.

With an inclination of his head and a swift unraveling of the tyrannous tongue, I was deposited onto the ground. *Beg your pardon, but what happened, Zammus? In truth, I've no idea! To start with, you are not at all in control. Whatever this being, this superior entity, wants or demands, it gets and you were never in control to begin with.*

"I know," I answered.

I lay silent, stretching out on the small black rocks that were subtly digging into my spine, not caring about the pain or being utterly immune, I was not sure. I allowed myself to view a blood dagger red sky. The behemoth beast beside me tucked his enormous, spiked head and serpentine neck into the concave region of his shoulder. Shaking the ground with his great bulk to comfort himself he lastly opened his wings and spread them over himself, tucking himself under their broad, ample membranes. A patch of orange wing entirely enclosed me in its warmth. Enjoying the agreeable warmth, but then remembering who it belonged to, I slithered away from its pleasant confines.

The ground hummed and deeply throbbed from the sonorous, bellowing breathing of this titan. Turning onto my right side away from the beast, I closed my eyes and was the second to be sucked into the vortex of sleep.

***

"UP! UP! UP! UP!" Sound exploded into my ears as grapeshot. Alert and shaking the exhaustion from my limbs, I stood onto my feet and found us fully surrounded by a phalanx of over five hundred in strength. W*hat the hell is this?! Where'd they come from?* The closest creature was four yards away and was hideously savage in appearance. Its torso was twice the size of my own and adorned in brown and stale green scales. Its chest split into two shoulders like a man's but, unlike any anatomy or physiological structure I had ever witnessed, two extra arms sprouted on each side of its ribcage. Its neck was thick and its head oval with two backward curving spines on the crown of its head. Its torso ended in a long ever-extending cord of flexible serpentine muscle. Four sheaths protruded over its shoulder blades, and they were all empty.

Bright slanted turquoise eyes regarded me with menacing aggression, yet their glare also consisted of sincere confusion. Dozens of the creatures were peering offensively at my companion and me. A red and orange sand-filled wind was blowing in far away from the right. The sand danced and leapt to-and-fro across the blades and spears of our assailants.

I was groping for the plate on my chest in order to produce the implausible strength that I would need to defeat or at least stand my ground against such a force. The plate with its godly power to transmute genetics and biology was gone!

"It's been gone," the dragon to my left proclaimed. "Ever since we first met."

Aghast, my knees buckled at how utterly defenseless I was. From the mass of serpentine warriors a long thick spear with wicked blades on either side was raised towards me and roughly embedded in the ground at my feet.

"A sense of honor! I don't understand!" I gawked.

The figure flicked out a forked purple tongue in response and produced four wicked outward-curving blades.

"You were only given that weapon so that these savages could further enjoy killing you. They enjoy a challenge." As the dragon was speaking, the horde of antagonists surged forward and hundreds of spears were let loose in our direction.

Shit, Zammus! It's us against these immeasurable odds! Into the halls of my demise; it's only time we say our good-byes. I shook my head at the incredulous nonsense my mind was spewing and, plucking the double-bladed spear from the ground, I marveled at its unlikely lightness. With much more accuracy then expected, I slashed open the stomach of one. Dodging its writhing body, I spun and impaled a leaping creature above me, its body fully uncoiled. The being went stiff and I immediately collapsed under its weight. The blade facing downwards sunk into my calf and I was struck in the chest with a spear and hurled backwards. My head hit the ground as I slid, and blood erupted from my mouth, gushing out of me and threatening to suffocate and drown me.

Zammus? A stiff serpentine warrior collapsed on top of me with enough force and velocity to shatter every bone and rupture the organs in my body. The shaft of the spear splintered, the blade piercing me even deeper.

"Yes?" I weakly rasped through a mouthful of blood.

Good-bye. I felt so weary and exhausted. Closing my eyes felt like the only good thing to do that would benefit me. The vibrations and heavy sounds of battle, the flapping of wings, the hissing of long blades through the air, the monstrous cacophony of reptilian roaring all ceased at once. Everything was frozen and I felt light! As light as the particles incessantly running rampant through the air. I experienced the sensation of traversing skywards. Nothing was moving. The mammoth form of the dragon revealed itself frozen in place with its gargantuan wings spread out beautifully, its talons inches from the ground, its tail coiled yet taut as its victim lay paralyzed by time.

Hundreds of spears lay buried in the air. The saliva of both the dragon and its enemies hung like droplets from their maws. A startled serpentine creature hung next to the forepaw of the dragon. The anatomical position of its claws clearly expressed that it had struck a physical blow to its foe and, due to the serpent's physical alignment, that blow had been effective. Peculiarly I felt myself being drawn closer and closer towards the dragon. I couldn't differentiate between feeling whether it was willingly or unwillingly. I disappeared into its muscular forearm, without any resistance. I felt very heavy all of a sudden and weighed down, yet I didn't at all feel unfamiliar.

Sound and hundreds of bodies burst into life all around me. *Fight them or leave? Fight them!* I roared. My left foreleg twisted and caught one of the monsters from its torso and sliced up to its neck. Flat pieces of steel struck me everywhere, but none were able to penetrate my scaly armor. Gliding to the left I snapped my wings shut and crawled onto the ground. The thick cord of my tail raced through the air and tossed several dozens of the four-armed savages onto the ground. *How to breathe fire? I don't know. Maybe it's as simple as thinking about it.* No flames bellowed from my jaws. Abandoning the thought and tilting my body, I spiraled into the air, steadying my form through leveling out my wings and glided very close to the ground.

The serpents fell as the edges of my wings slit their more susceptible scaly armor. Speeding through disorganized ranks and their ineffective arms of war, I grabbed a dozen in each forepaw and, pumping my wings furiously, rose in height. My talons loosened and, thrashing wildly and screaming, my enemies descended to their deaths. With the whip of my tail, swords of my wings, and impenetrable armor of my scales I fought, defended, and attacked for a period vacant of time.

***

I struck out with my tail which rapidly uncoiled with a flick. The air parted and collapsed under the blow. My claws lashed out. *Nothing!* I acutely spun and jabbed with a wing thrust. *Nothing?!* Spinning around I met only an orange and brown plain that lay still as death. Looking down and around I saw why. The landscape was swelling with freshly ravaged *"S"* and *"L"* shaped corpses. They were everywhere! Under my talons, scattered in heaps, some isolated, others relaxed and spread out in neat and shabby rows. The serpent corpses had been brutally produced. Many heads, tails, arms, and torsos had been dismembered, even their elongated four-digit claws. Sapphire blood had filthily mixed with the ground.

"Yes, you killed them all," A familiar voice suddenly intoned.

I found myself being ejected from the dragon's mouth all of a sudden. *Hey! Where am I going?! What's happening!*

"Out. You're getting out," spoke the voice that I now recognized as the dragon's. "Wait for it, it shouldn't take long," it growled.

From the pile of serpent corpses, a much smaller shape freed itself and at rapid speed propelled itself in my direction. Two long spears had mutilated its form. One had skewered the humanoid torso whilst another had obliterated its lower leg.

"Hey, that's me! That's mine! It's me!" I yelled.

"Yes," hummed the dragon.

How can that be me, though? My body is right here, I thought, looking down. I didn't see any flesh, though. To my horror and further confusion all I saw was a pale grayish-white stream of vapor. I didn't have much time to stare and ponder. The moment I looked up I was pierced hard by a physical mass. The next thing I knew is that I could feel. A split second later a limitless and unbearable pain exploded everywhere in the shattered husk that was my body. I screamed and collapsed, wailing and sobbing through the implausible pain. My chest and leg blazing like a forest fire and at the same time frozen with crippling frostbite like the arctic. I whimpered and bit down on my lip hard, viciously drawing blood.

"I'm broken! What am I even doing here?" I cried.

For the first time the dragon didn't respond. I yelped and savagely ground my teeth together as I felt my leg and chest bones horrifically grind and shift, rearranging themselves. As my piercing wails rose, they were met by the sound of two boulders screeching against each other. Everything went black.

***

I awoke to shocking painlessness. Yawning I stretched my arms and blinked several times. I wasn't in that frightening orange desert surrounded by serpent corpses anymore. I shuddered at the thought, never wanting to revisit that memory, but knowing it would haunt my dreams for a long, long time. I was in an empty blue field. The dragon was not too far off with his back turned to me.

"Where are we?" I asked.

"In the Asgari Hills," replied the dragon, still not facing me.

"I need answers. To everything," I proclaimed.

"Very well," agreed the dragon, turning to face me. "First off you're dead."

"What? Did I hear right? What!?" I blinked.

"Your body does not exist on any visible plane."

I couldn't move as his words continued to paralyze me and sap my strength. The little comfort and temporal ease I had were vanishing.

The dragon continued, "This form I now have is not present in the material world–"

"What? How!" I interrupted.

Powerful and authoritative eyes narrowed dangerously. "I will refuse to share my knowledge with you if you don't cease your incessant tumult of questions!" lashed the dragon.

I gulped and remained motionless in both body and mind.

Flicking its barbed tail casually over its left side it proceeded. "Both you and I lack a presence in the corporeal dimension. Due to my ancient age and powers of the flame, I am able to perceive what is happening to you in the physical world. You lack a body. The ancient device that enables you to transmute your lesser flesh into fire-filled reptilian that grants you vast levels of strength you have yet to even tap into is known as the Anura. There were once many. You had the last one which has now concealed itself, and it can only be drawn forth if it so wishes. Millions of years ago during the peak of the ancient wars, this world of flames was failing against an undefeatable omnipotence that was not from here. Those millions years past were the only times in Terra Draco's history when all the races renounced their multitudes of hatred for each other and banded together for survival.

"The ten-legged sand dwellers burrowed to our aid and made vast tunneling systems that were as wide as mountains. The four-armed serpents taught us their arts of weapon forging and slithery combat, while our two-legged cousins the prugalas gave us brute force, muscle, and endless endurance with their sand-wielding abilities. Legions of behemoth magma centipedes massacred our enemies; dra-kin allowed us the advantage of both terrain and aerial combat; and the Stone Walkers of Flame that haven't been seen for millions of years aided us with their malleable fire abilities. Even with all this force and power, we were being slaughtered by the billions every single day. Our most elite flame practitioners found and forged our salvation. The Anura; a tool solely created to intensify the strength, power, endurance, speed, and energy of its user to godly levels.

"It was a weapon, a means that could give anyone the impossible strength to level a mountain to fragments with the lightest blow. Or the ability for ten warriors alone to decimate a swarm of trillions in one day. The Anuras are how we won the war and with them we imprisoned Terra Draco's oldest enemy, Maldroto, in the fiery bowels of the planet's innermost core. After the war our home was battle scarred, an oblivion. All six races had used the Anuras and all six of us feared them. Through a pact that had to be formed, they were declared infernal. No one had to say it or argue that if 'We kept the tools of our salvation that granted us liberation, through lust, greed, and power they would lead to our last hour and our total damnation.' So we destroyed them all. And we obliterated those of us who disagreed.

"The only Anura that could not be destroyed was the first one ever made. The Crown Anura. And only one knew of its existence because they had created it. I made it. And it was different than all the thousands that followed. The Crown Anura had a life force and a sentience where the others did not. The Crown was forged to destroy Maldroto and obliterate him entirely. The others were created to defeat him and rob him of his power. Due to the life force that the Crown Anura had, I never activated it, because I knew that it could corrupt me. It was never used in the wars. The Anuras that were applied in the wars were able to be destroyed because they fulfilled their existence. As the maker I would not and fortunately I could not be the one to carry out this task. The

Anura needed me and I had to protect my world. I could not leave so intelligent a being and so lethal a weapon on Terra Draco due to the risk that it could be found by anyone and lead to this world's inevitable destruction.

"I forsook my mate Mvellara and my entire life, so that Terra Draco could exist. I consulted in the Anura and expressed my infinite concerns. Together we found a solution. The Anura would leave our world and search for an executor of its will in peace if I allowed myself to fuse temporarily with its essence. I complied. Two things and two things only have occurred over the billions of years since I, the dragon named Jaow-kieen, ended my existence on Terra Draco, my home. First, I traveled in the small disk of the Anura, where I agreed to have my soul momentarily confined. Together we traversed an immeasurable plentitude of stars in search of one who would wield the Anura and fulfill its purpose. Second, the Anura shared with me everything regarding its knowledge and intelligence that I was not aware of, the most important being that the Crown Anura, my eternal companion, was made with the genetic and spiritual properties of all the six races of Terra Draco.

"The wielder would have to unite all six of these races to destroy Maldroto. To accomplish this, they would have all six of these groups' individual properties and advantages. Their mind would be destroyed and this world would fall in the process of placing Maldroto into the void," the dragon finished.

I didn't move or speak for a very long time.

"Why did it choose me out of all the infinite worlds and individuals to carry out this task!" I yelled. "Why!"

"The Anura has a mind and will of its own. It conducted the great search, I was just a passenger. It always confided its thoughts with me honestly and genuinely, just as it responded to my own. I myself have asked it a hundred thousand times, 'Why choose his world? Why him? What's in any of them?' The Anura always replied in the same tone, 'He and his world are perfect candidates because out of infinite fairness and probability they were chosen. Not by preference nor disdain, but countless odds and possibility. This means that had your world not been chosen, another being from another would have just as equal a chance and likelihood of having been selected to become the wielder and successfully fulfill my existence.' Whether you like it or not, Zammus, you became the wielder of the Crown Anura the moment you picked it up in its disguised form as a jeweled ornament from that treasure hoard on that island on your world.

"The Anura coalesced into your essence in the physical world, and that's why you and I are occupying this parallel mirror reality. In the physical world you currently exist as a pile of red burnt scales lying dormant at the bottom of a molten river. To return to the physical world to fulfill your tasks as the wielder, you must be trained by me physically, mentally, emotionally, and spiritually to be strong enough. There are three entities; the Anura, myself, and you, Zammus. When your training is complete and you are strong enough to enter and exist in the physical world, the memories and life forces of the Crown Anura, my dragon essence, and your mind, Zammus, will be fused. All this knowledge will be yours to call upon readily and freely. You will have a mind that is billions of years old," the dragon's jaws snapped shut.

"That's enough for one day. I'm going to rest." Jaow-kieen announced.

His wings formed a dome over his body and concealed all of him, except his reddish golden snout and tail. I was paralyzed. *What do I do? What can I even do? Where do I even start?*

"Even though training technically started when we first met, you didn't know it. I was just getting a feel for your mind. The official training begins at dawn before any of the five suns rise. Sleep, Zammus," Jaow-kieen spoke.

"Good night," I replied. There was no visible moon I could see, only complete darkness. I stood up determined to accomplish something and foolishly sat down just as quickly, not knowing what to do.

"I'm trapped. I don't want this. I can't do this," I said to myself.

There is nothing you can do to alter or escape from this situation, said my inner voice.

"I want to run away," I whispered furiously.

And go where?

"I will run away," I spoke.

You need a place to run off to, challenged my thoughts.

"There is nothing, but death, desolation, and despair here on this path," I sulked.

With melancholy my thoughts replied, *Death, desolation and despair are everywhere. On all paths.*

"Not for everyone and not all get administered the same dosage!" I argued stubbornly.

Everyone does not apply to you, spoke my thoughts.

"I'm quite literally the only one of my kind here," I lamented.

You are the only human on this world. None of the reptilian monsters like you. You have no friends here and it will always remain so. If you stay with the dragon or take your leave, you die here anyways. Death will take you regardless of what you do. It's inevitable. There is no point in pondering your meaningless fate, explained my thoughts.

"That's not fair! None of this is fair!" I protested.

Life isn't fair. No one gets everything they want, my thoughts reminded me.

"I'm going to sleep," I announced, tired of this stupid and pointless debate, tired of being here, tired of everything, tired of living and existence itself.

Sleep is good, agreed my thoughts, *For now.*

Sleep if it could be called that, was horrible, I had the same horrifically gruesome nightmare over and over and over again. I was in the dragon arena where the Anura accidentally transformed my flesh. I was in my regular form, the body I had been born with and the only one I had had for twenty-five years. My black hair was long, braided, and shoulder length; my skin was bare and looked just as it always had, tanned dark to a teak brown. The Anura was not on my chest or anywhere to be seen. A shadow passed over me as a silver-scaled dragon scooped me up in its talons. I didn't scream; there was nothing I could do and my emotions were deadened.

My captor seemed to be hundreds of feet above the ground. With artistic grace its talons released me. I was falling. A jade-colored dragon appeared in midair right in front of me, jaws agape. Red-orange flames spiraled from its maw and bathed me. Cooked to a stiff charcoal black shell, I still breathed. I felt another dragon come. Sapphire blue flames engulfed my burnt flesh. Though I don't know how, I saw my burnt, crispy, oil black body totally consumed by blue fire until only the white bones remained. Even though I had no body to physically perceive any sensations, I felt that I did. I felt that I was an invisible force that was everywhere all at once. I inexplicably was detached from my body while at the same connected and whole. I felt infinite pain, heat, and sorrow. Using invisible, inexplicable, and nonexistent eyes, I watched a red and gold dragon, Jaow-kieen, swoop in with mammoth wings and vaporize my skeleton with white flames.

By means unknown to myself I felt it all, though physically it wasn't at all possible. I relived this hell dozens of times throughout the night.

Sprack! Sprack! Sprack!

"Get up, Zammus! Official training begins today!" chorused Jaow-kieen as he whipped his tail against the rocky ground.

Screaming and hollering in horror I yelled, "Get away from me! Right now! Leave me alone!"

Up on my feet I ran for it, not knowing where to, but away from here. To my horror I heard Jaow-kieen open his wings. He grabbed me in his talons and ignored my screams and shouts which grew louder and louder.

"Put me down! Let me go, now! I HATE YOU!"

We landed on a plateau. I jumped for it.

"That's not going to fix it or do anything or improve your mood. You're not in the physical world, Zammus! Same rules don't apply!" he yelled.

I hit the ground and destroyed not a single bone, muscle, or fiber in my body. Unimaginably disappointed and depressed I just lay there on my stomach. Jaow-kieen came down.

"I told you jumping off the cliff wouldn't make you feel better or put an end to your miserable troubles. This is not the physical world you and I are inhabiting, Zammus. There are a very different set of rules. Now please tell me, what is the matter? What is wrong?"

"Everything. This whole place. Don't you understand? Everything. Every. Single. Thing," I moped.

"I understand you," Jaow-kieen sighed.

"You do?" I asked, intrigued.

"Better than anyone you'll meet. I've suffered depression, insomnia, anxiety, isolation and post-traumatic stress disorder for millions and billions of years. When you live as I do time becomes impossible. It doesn't exist and mentally one's mind cannot compute it. Eons become months, millennia become weeks, centuries flow as days, and decades pass by in hours. Sometimes I've suffered the disorders of a deteriorating mind all at once and other times each individual illness milks my consciousness. How long have you existed, Zammus?" asked Jaow-kieen.

"Twenty-five years," I answered.

"Your experience compared to mine is smaller than the tiniest grain of sand and as fresh and green as a newly birthed cell that is a fraction of a second old. You can't complain. One day is nothing to me. I will observe your sorrow with you for the passing of one day. Tomorrow will be the latest that we start. Fair?"

"Thank you," I said.

Jaow-kieen sat by me and spread a wing over me to protect me from the suns. There we sat comfortable in silence, never needing to break its peace.

***

I awoke to the sight of Jaow-kieen's enormous golden yellow eye looking at me from a small distance away.

"I feel great! What happened to me?" I proclaimed, jumping onto my feet with supple strength, vigor, and energy.

"You slept for seven days and seven nights."

"Wow! What? How?!" I spasmed. "Hmmphh! I definitely required such rest! Do we start forging me into the warrior I must become or what?" I grinned. *Hmph, hmmm. Well, that's a bizarre change of heart. Doesn't sound genuine. At all,* my mind opined. *Look,* I responded, *Listen, I know that this is completely delusional thinking, but what else am I supposed to do? I guess just mold myself to the dictates of this reality,* I thought somberly. *Well,* the other part of me said, trailing off.

"Yes. Your training will consist of four areas. Your soul, emotional well-being, mental capacity, and physical capability. All four of these parts of you will be strengthened to levels beyond that of apex elite ability. The first part of your training will revolve around physical conditioning," Jaow-kieen looked down at me from his long neck.

"Your strength compared to the weakest creature on this planet is like a grain of sand and a mountain. We have a lot of work to do–"

"I can't get that strong! Maybe you reptiles have completely different genetic muscular potential, but humans physically cannot attain such godly amounts of muscle and strength! It's totally impossible!" I argued.

"You will discover the truth. The Anura you will find naturally grants you levels of vast superior strength. Its fiery energy is being produced and regulated in every nucleus of every one of your cells as we speak," spoke Jaow-kieen.

"Incredible! And equally unbelievable! I'm curious, though. When Dar Vagoue, my prugala friend, first met me and we fought, he was stronger than me, but his strength is not unattainable for me to reach, is it?" I asked.

"Zammus, the strongest prugalas on this planet are seven to twelve times stronger than your prugala friend, so that's a muscular runt of his species. And you are five to seven times weaker than him. Understand?"

"Oh," I said. "How do you know all that, though?" I asked.

"Climb up on my back," Jaow-kieen ordered, not answering the question. I did as I was told.

"Where are we going?" I asked, seated between two tall spines.

"You'll see," was his reply.

Shortly after, we landed in a rocky area where pillars of brown and black stone grew out of the ground like fingers. All of them grew taller than any trees on earth. The vertical rocky structures also grew horizontal, connecting the pillars to each other through enormous bridges, like a giant web. Turning my head in all directions I saw that this rocky network of pillars and bridges spanned for countless miles. My breath was taken away at this marvelous, extraordinary, and completely unimaginable feat of architecture.

"This is where you will train," confirmed Jaow-kieen. "I want you to climb that pillar. All of these structures have countless grooves on their surface, suitable for climbing," Jaow-kieen pointed with his tail at a rocky column to the right of us.

“And what do I do once I finish?”

“We’ll worry about that after, once you start and finish climbing,” he replied.

I looked at the task before me. The rocky indentations started at the base by my feet and covered every inch of the pillar like scales. Looking up I saw that it reached seemingly endlessly into the sky. I placed my feet on the lowest grooves and reached up and grabbed a ledge. I pulled myself up and my toes and fingernails found new places.

“What happens if I fall?”

“Don’t worry, you won’t.”

Jaow-kieen was wrong, after what seemed like twenty minutes my fingers, arms, toes and legs were burning and I lost my grip screaming. Before I could even descend a couple inches Jaow-kieen rushed up from below me and I fell softly on gold and red copper-colored wings. He tilted his body towards the pillar.

“Jump off and continue as you were,” Jaow-kieen spoke gently.

I found my grip and proceeded. I reached the top in what felt like two and a half hours. In total I lost my grip and fell five times, but due to Jaow-kieen’s protective nature he always made sure I started where I left off, unharmed. Pulling myself up onto the top of the pillar I rolled over onto my back and closed my eyes, utterly spent. I felt Jaow-kieen settle besides me.

“Well done. After an hour’s rest you will do two hundred vertical body pulls by hanging off the bridge next to us,” said Jaow-kieen.

“What?! Two hundred?! Of what?” I gaped.

Jaow-kieen snorted. “Are you not acquainted with the anatomical position where the body is hanging vertically on a ledge by its arms, to be precise its hands, and it pulls itself up until its chin is over the ledge through contracting the biceps, triceps, and back musculature?"

"Yes. Us humans call those pull-ups. Why must I do two hundred? I'm tired and I'm starving! Can I get a break?" I complained stubbornly.

"Due to it being your first day, I will lower it down to fifty. The essence of the Anura that flows through your veins will feed you and provide you with endless nutrients from the fire that is reproducing in your cells."

"Ughhh," I moaned. "Wake me in an hour, please."

"Affirmative, Zammus."

My rest was uneventful. I no longer felt hungry, but my arm and legs were aching.

"After you do your pull-ups, we shall go for a walk and we shall then train in combat and we shall eat something, alright?" announced Jaow-kieen with deep bellowing noises that had to be laughter.

The word 'food' jolted me to my senses. I did my pull-ups in five sets of ten in about twenty-five minutes. My arms felt like heavy pieces of stone that I couldn't even move.

"You'll need to get faster at doing those. I've seen baby prugalas do five times as much in five times as little time! Come, Zammus, we shall walk."

I ignored his comment and walked at his side. "What is this place and where is it? Does it exist outside of this spiritual bubble we're in?" I asked.

"You're so hasty for answers, Zammus! In time. In time," replied Jaow-kieen.

We both walked in silence. My eyes traced and darted over the grid system of horizontal and vertical roads of stone that looked like they ended and began nowhere.

"Hurry up! We're almost there!" called Jaow-kieen.

I hadn't even realized I was lagging. I ran up to him and beheld a giant stone disc that was neatly supported by five pillars, four on the sides and one in the center. The whole platform had to be about the size of a small island. There was a black dome in the center.

"The goal is simple. Under the obsidian covering lies food and provisions. Reach the dome and you can eat. If you can't reach it for whatever reason, then you'll have to find something else. You may need this," Jaow-kieen smirked as he slid me a rod of blue krystal.

"I don't need this," I said leaving the shaft on the floor.

"Are you sure?"

"Yes."

And with that I sprinted towards the dome, even though my calf muscles were screaming. In a flash of red and gold I was thrown back to the edge of the circle.

"To get to the dome, Zammus, you need to either stop or outsmart the dragon that is in the way. Perhaps you may find that stick handy about now," gloated Jaow-kieen.

"Damn it, Jaow-kieen."

My hand wrapped tightly around the blue baton and I ran to meet him. With a flick of his wing he deposited me high in the air and I landed hard with my arms and legs spread before me. As usual, physical pain did not exist here. When I got up Jaow-kieen was nowhere to be seen. I picked up my staff and slowly and cautiously walked with my weapon held high. I was halfway from the dome when his tail struck me like a bolt of lightning.

My body flew well over the rim of the platform and I struck one of the columns.

"I should be dead, Jaow-kieen! My body should be torn to splinters! I miss seeing my blood! I miss feeling pain!" I yelled. "This isn't right! This isn't fair!"

"Yeah, yeah, yeah! Just focus on reaching that dome," spoke Jaow-kieen, startling me.

"How'd you get here?" I spun wildly.

He swooped me up in his claws, beat his wings, and in a burst of light I was back at square one holding my staff.

"Come on, Zammus! Reach the dome!" commanded Jaow-kieen.

We played this horrific game for hours until it got dark. I was thrown into the air, off the platform, into stone pillars thousands of times. And I was no closer to achieving my aim than when I started.

This is like expecting a rock to suddenly sprout legs and turn into a turtle! I thought bitterly. I was forced by Jaow-kieen to watch him greedily and rather sloppily slurp up whatever was in the dome. And yet again by his force he refused to even show me what the contents were.

"I'll warn you only once, if you try to sneak into this place and find out what is under the dome without my presence, I will find you, remove you from this location, and abandon you. Forever. You'll never see me or the physical world ever again."

"Understood," I gulped in fear.

Damn! My thoughts echoed.

My skin started to feel very hot all of a sudden as if a heat wave was passing through.

"Look at your flesh. The Anura's powers, your newfound powers, are feeding you with nourishment and energy."

Once again, red-orange pathways were trailing up and across my arms, chest, stomach, back, legs, hands, and feet. I was lost staring at the multitude of flaming highways. I put my fingers on one of the trails. Molten energy pooled around it.

"How come I can't feel it or get burned?" I asked.

"Because you're made of fire now. Blood no longer flows through your body or makes up your cells. Fire does. Look closely at your body and you'll see," Jaow-kieen explained.

I looked at my chest and I saw the coiled shapes of my heart, lungs, liver, stomach, intestines, and kidneys all glowing orange through my skin. I could make out the fine, winding details of these flaming organs. I then looked at my arm and saw veins, arteries, and striped muscle tissue layer under layer in precise detail raging red and orange with my newfound fire. With new blazing life.

"So, if I bleed that's what comes out of me?"

"Yes," the dragon replied.

"Well, I hope it burns whoever drew it out."

"That's not how it works," Jaow-kieen said.

"What do you mean?"

"The only fire that is potent enough to be deadly are the flames that wrap around and naturally coat the ten feet of the sandfoots, dragon fire, and the fire that emits from the auríls' stone bodies. And the auríls, which reside in the Rek' Rast Magma Mountains, put that same fire in their fire-operated weapons."

"Hmmm. I see," I grunted, taking this in.

After this most bizarre and novel spectacle Jaow-kieen lead me to a bowl-shaped structure that sat atop a pillar like a wine goblet. The indentation was the size of a cabin. My eyes identified the scale-like protrusions that grew on all the pillars that would allow me to climb out of the bowl.

"This is where you shall have your privacy. Rest and gather your strength. Tomorrow we begin defensive combat."

"Very well. Good night, Jaow-kieen."

"Rest well in return, Zammus."

My dreams were not pleasant or negative. I was in a dark space and blinded by black fog or mist that I could not escape, no matter how fast I ran or which direction I went.

"Up, Zammus! Up! Up! Up!" Jaow-kieen yelled as his tail rattled against the outside of my bowl-shaped chamber.

Knowing that he would pry me out with his talons if I refused, I quickly climbed out.

"I took it you slept well," spoke my mentor.

"No, not one bit."

"Walk with me. Yesterday you trained in offensive combat by having to take something from me while I guarded it. Whether you succeeded or not was of no consequence. I had you play the role of an invasive force that entered my territory, the disc platform, to conduct a mission to seize and utilize my assets. In the context of yesterday that would be touching the black dome to become the owner of its contents. Today you defend yourself against one of the six races whose only purpose is to kill you," explained Jaow-kieen.

"Great," I said. "Do I get my staff from yesterday?"

"No. I want you to use what's around you. You won't always have a physical weapon in every fight, but you will always enter each one with your mind," said Jaow-kieen.

I sighed, lamenting. The both of us were now on the network of bridges that flowed from the pillars.

"Sandfoot up ahead! Brace yourself!" warned Jaow-kieen as he leapt with open wings and disappeared upwards, "I'll be here where it's safe!"

"Thanks," I growled.

A tortoise-like beast that had to be about the size of a large carriage was charging towards me. The dark red and orange flames that covered its ten paws left scorch marks on the bridge's surface. The horns on its shoulders and head were positioned for stabbing!

"Zammus, how are we going to get ourselves out of this one?" I said aloud.

The sandfoot thrust its horns at my body. My eyes closed in anticipation. Like a musket ball my body was shot and propelled off the side of the bridge. As I fell through the air I felt the horns of my pursuer pierce and pass through my left arm and shoulder. Howling just like an animal, I watched liquid flames gush out of me. The sandfoot twisted its head and plucked its horns out of me, my fiery flesh clinging to them. Twisting its head back again it clamped a pair of beak-like jaws onto the back of my right thigh. It chewed me viciously and all I could do was scream in pain and terror amidst the hopelessness of the situation.

"JAOW-KIEEN! HELP!" I roared in agony.

Glop!

"AEGHHH-URGCHHHHH!!!!"

The creature's beak snapped down hard through the bone of my femur.

"JAOW-KIEEN! PLEASE!" I begged, sobbing.

In a rush of wings and claws Jaow-kieen ripped my attacker off of me and threw it into the maze of columns and bridges below where it crumbled into dust. Catching me gently, he gathered me in his paw and deposited me on the wide flat top of a pillar.

"I thought I wasn't able to . . . feel . . . pain," I cried choking on my tears. "Why did you do this to me, Jaow-kieen? Why?"

"You will not die. It's not possible at least here. I must accelerate your healing. There is nothing I can say or do to prepare you for what's about to happen," Jaow-kieen said.

"What?" I sobbed.

Through my watery vision I saw him open his jaws wider than I had ever seen before. Red and orange flames spiraled out of his maw and bathed me entirely. My lungs and diaphragm exploded as I experienced pain that I didn't think was ever even possible. My vision went utterly black for several long moments and then it fragmented into bursts of color. I was aware of smoke rising off of my body. I couldn't move; shock, paralysis, and petrifaction were all understatements. So was cerebral impairment. Jaow-kieen looked at me with worry and concern. My brain couldn't compute. My brain was exhausted and spent. My mind had been ravaged and my emotions raped and butchered without end.

"Zammus?" asked Jaow-kieen.

"I thought we were friends," I said shakily getting to my feet.

"I am," he replied.

"If you were, you would not have allowed what happened to me to happen. You put me in these circumstances. You can't be my friend."

"But Zammus?" implored the dragon.

"YOU ARE NOT MY FRIEND! I'm going to get my staff and leave this place," I proclaimed coldly.

"You can't!"

"Watch me!"

"You don't understand, Zammus! The Crown Anura's presence on this world is slowly weakening Maldroto's bonds of imprisonment so he can escape, therefore allowing the wielder to inevitably fulfill the Anura's sole purpose. If you don't stay here, then you doom our world. Maldroto will annihilate this world with his poison seed, and he won't fail this time. Terra Draco will fall and die! Everything will be lost and destroyed. All life forms and the fire that fuels and sustains this place," Jaow-kieen beseeched.

"This is not my world! Its problems are not my concern! So leave me ALONE!" I lashed in utter rage.

Turning my back on him I leapt onto a bridge several paces away. I worked my legs into a run.

"Maldroto will escape!" yelled Jaow-kieen.

My legs responded by pounding the stone faster, set on finding the disc island platform where we trained yesterday.

"Maldroto will escape!" roared the dragon even louder in anguish, despair and desperation.

I never heard him follow behind me. I ran up and down the bridges and searched the tops of the columns that connected them. Eventually I found the disc platform. There it lay majestically; a circle of flat stone broader than any field I had ever seen in Europe and wider than any arena I had seen or read about in history books. The imperial and majestic circle was supported by those five godly pillars. Dashing across the bridge leading to it I quickly leapt onto its rim. I spotted my sapphire krystal staff. Having recovered it, I looked at the black obsidian dome and thought of disobeying Jaow-kieen and looking at its contents. Thinking the better of it, I ran past the dome. Off the rim of the platform, into the network of bridges and columns of stone.

I know not how long I ran through there, leapt onto bridges, and glided past pillars. Eventually when the sky was almost dark and the five suns were low I had to rest. I bet I had run only a tenth of this entire place. I sat down with my back against a pillar and the rest of my body on a bridge, and I cried. Looking at the multitude of bridges below me I wondered, *How far is it until the bottom?*

Go find out, my mind responded. This time I didn't argue with myself.

"Yes, let us find out," I said aloud.

I stood up and walked to the edge of the bridge.

"That's a long fall," I said.

"I know," I replied.

"I hope I don't survive it," I answered.

"I hope it kills you too," I agreed.

"To death," I grinned broadly.

"To death." I raised my arm in reply and stepped off.

I saw very few bridges as I fell and this delighted me. But everything was going by really fast and a bridge was coming up quickly ahead. This fact and inevitable prospect greatly disappointed me. I bounced as my ribs hit the stone with enough force that would have shattered the hardest of rocks. There I lay physically intact, but internally shattered and destroyed beyond repair. I cried all the more that my suicide jump had not relieved and saved me. And then she suddenly filled my thoughts after all this time and encroached on my mind, completely uninvited. Memories of the past trespassed through my brain. Images of a life that could have been, now a life perpetually lost flowed into my consciousness.

VALAURA!

I hated what was happening to me now. I hated that I was doing this to myself. I hated myself for putting myself through this. But I could think of nothing else. There was nothing else to think about. But the past. My past. The worst and saddest part of it all, though, was that since being out at sea and even after all that had happened since I came here, wherever here was, she hadn't been on my mind at all. Not once! It's as if I had completely forgotten her. And even worse than that, I hadn't even noticed. *How? Why?* My mind fumbled feebly trying to catch the fading whisps and specters.

***

Valaura Elyiscea, daughter of the House of Droeburg of London, England. March 24th, 1655. Thursday.

"Wasn't Freddy's wedding a spectacle of rapture, darling?" expressed my fiancé.

"Yes, of course! I wish your brother, the prince, and his beloved wife Catherina lovely days of prosperous wealth and overflowing happiness. The day of our own nuptials will be approaching in a fortnight, my dearest sapphire blossom," I purred, wrapping my arms around Valaura's waist.

"Oh, Zammus Dre' Suel of Welkenshire! Your words are warm mellifluous notes and the heart within my breast an instrument of chords!" she exclaimed, placing her sweet nectar-scented face on my neck.

"As long as you allow me to tune and play your strings, my queen," I smirked, cupping her face in my hand and tilting her chin upward.

"Stroke my strings, you prodigious musician! Express your passion through my body. Make me sing. Let us make the greatest music together!" she squealed as her soft lips met my own and imparted upon them many melodies.

Not long after we rode in a private carriage on the way to our home. The cushions and walls of the carriage were a lovely shade of black, but the full moon painted them bone white.

"I'm most tired, darling," Valaura sighed softly.

I put my arm around her so that her head rested on my shoulder.

"Here's a pillow, dear. The ride is only an hour. I'll wake you when we arrive," I said, kissing her gently on her forehead. My lips tenderly lingered there momentarily.

"Mmph. Thank you," she moaned softly.

"I wonder where I'll have to take our crew next, Captain Pierce. I'm just delighted that this mission will be short. One week going. One coming back," I whispered.

I procured a small journal from my coat pocket and began the daily ritual of recording my experiences.

Today I woke before the dawn at four a.m. From that time until six I cultivated my spirit through meditation. From six until ten I peacefully slept alongside Valaura's lovely essence. I recall a strange, yet humorous dream involving a rhinoceros and grass. I was a brown and black rhinoceros grazing off the long wild grasses of Africa when suddenly a voice spoke, startling me.

"Why must you insist on chewing me the way you do? Has it never occurred to you that I, the grass, and my green brethren don't like you and your kind eating us? Have you ever given an inkling of thought to this ethical and moral regard?"

"Who said that?!" I yelped.

"Down here, you horned buffoon!"

"Where?" I panicked, stomping my rhinoceros' feet.

"Everywhere! I'm all around you, you fool! The grass! I am the grass!"

I did what any sensible creature would do. I ran! As fast as my four legs could take me. Green blades and shoots of grass erupted from the soil and shot towards me. I had woken up screaming in horror and convulsions. Eventually Valaura's tender embraces and sweet-song voice had calmed me.

The ink from my quill smeared as the driver abruptly tugged on the reins of the shire horses.

"Blast it, William! You must deploy more ease when you slow steeds! Damn it, man!" I swore under my breath.

I turned over and looked at Valaura's calm features and motionless countenance.

"You could sleep through anything my dear, even an earthquake or a flood."

I sealed my inkwell and replaced it, the quill and journal tucked into the pockets of my royal navy-blue coat. Upon exiting the carriage, I gathered Valaura in my arms.

"Please attend to Miss Elyiscea's luggage, Mr. Withersby."

"Aye."

We had no difficulties getting into our household, except a slightly minor dilemma involving me having to hand William the keys to the house from my coat pockets whilst I held my betrothed in both arms.

"Thank you, William for as always ensuring our safety when we're on the road and being a responsible and trustworthy driver who ensures a harmless passage for his family. You've always been a good man," I spoke.

"You have always treated me with the utmost respect, kindness and fairness of heart for all the twenty-two years that we've known each other, brother," replied William.

"Brother . . ." I intoned. "Rest well."

"May your slumber be sweet as nectar, Zammus!"

"Nectar?!" I grinned.

"We've always had a pompous way with these jesting formalities and silly unnecessary titles, haven't we?" he smirked.

Abruptly we both burst into laughter at the ludicrousness of our farce.

"Rest you well on this night," I smiled after it subsided, giving a slight bow.

"Rest you well," my brother bowed back.

I carried Valaura up the spiraling staircase to our bedroom. I gently lay the heart and soul of my life on our bed. With gentle and delicate ease, I removed her booted high heels and let her be. Having put them against the wall of our dresser I sat on my end of the bed and removed my own boots. The white orb of the moon's full radiance engulfed the entirety of the room as it bled through the circular window. I walked over to the window and with my arms clasped behind my back I took in the sight of the vast forest below. The moon's rays soaked the needles of the pines and firs like fresh milk. I turned and looked to Valaura's illuminated features.

The moonlight displayed her normally chestnut brown hair as blonde and the small amount of freckles she had stuck out in beauteous stark contrast. I lay down beside her and fell fast asleep.

***

Unconsciously or consciously my mind shut off the memories.

"No more flashbacks. Back to the torture cell," I said to myself as two large tears rolled down my cheeks. "Jaow-kieen, training, death, Maldroto, focus," I forced myself to speak.

I took a deep breath and, with my eyes still closed, counted to my favorite number, seventeen. Ever so slowly I opened them and immediately spied the sapphire krystal staff a small distance away to my right side. I erected my body into a squatting crouch. I counted another repetition of seventeen breaths. I stood up and walked over to the staff. *This wasn't here earlier. It must have fallen from the higher levels after I jumped,* I thought.

My fingers closed around the jagged contours of the staff and a blue light radiated around me. I tried to fling the rod away from me; yet, to my horror, it remained steadfast to my hand. Thick blue misty liquid flowed violently out of the staff. Screaming, I pulled on it with my other hand, only for it to become glued to the shaft by some invisible supernatural adhesive. The blue essence congealed into a globular clump that floated into the air as it evaporated from my hands. The mass stretched itself, wobbled, and bobbed like an animal. Pinpricks of turquoise light shot out like arrows from the blue mass as it juddered violently.

The clump swelled and swelled as it flared brighter and scorched the air around me. I shielded my face in my arms anticipating the violent explosion as the orb burned white. Nothing struck me. No heat or wave of violent energy. Hesitantly I opened my eyes and watched as the orb, now back to its original dark blue, elongated itself into the shape of a tall, well figured, and robust woman. Her dark blue bare skin glowed like polished metal and shimmered like a gemstone.

"I am the Crown Anura," the woman announced in a soft, even, mellifluous voice.

I lowered my head, staring at the ground, my eyes and face not worthy to experience and behold her godly cosmic beauty.

"I'm . . . I'm–Za–," I choked on my words.

"Zammus Dre' Suel, your eyes are more than worthy to look upon me. I chose you. You are the second entity that I have permitted myself to be shown to and that I too have seen since I was forged by my father, Jaow-kieen, billions or trillions of years ago."

I raised my head and beheld her unbelievably flawless, perfect, and radiant features. Her eyes glowed a mesmerizing sky blue.

"Do you have a name that you prefer to be called? Crown Anura makes you sound like an object or some tool to be used. I don't see you like that nor can I perceive you to be as such."

"That's quite flattering and philosophical of you to say. Well, Jaow-kieen, who's both my father and my best friend–well, my only friend actually–calls me An-u. You too may call me that."

"An-u," I repeated. "No disrespect to your father and my mentor, but he's so very blunt, straightforward, stubborn, and unrelenting at times."

"Oh, I know that for certain!" she grinned.

"But he is also very protective," I said honestly.

"He is. Want to take a walk with me?" she offered.

"Sure. I'm just curious though. How did you find my old home and how long were you there waiting?"

An-u's body shimmered as she lost a couple of inches in height until we were both as tall as one another.

"What was that for?" I asked.

"Well, how else was I supposed to know how tall you were!"

"In truth I feel much more comfortable talking to you like that now and not having to stare up at you like a god figure."

She filled the air with her laughter. "To answer your questions, Zammus, we searched endlessly for the right type of individual–"

"Wait a second!" I cut her off. "Right type of individual? Jaow-kieen told me that I was picked at random. And that any being from any world would have been just as equally qualified," I spoke completely confused.

"I don't know about that. Maybe that's how he interpreted it. I did the choosing, not him. I know what Terra Draco needs."

I was shocked by her words and her way of thinking.

Disagree with Jaow-kieen, I thought to myself. *His very own daughter! The Anura!*

"To answer your second question, I waited in that treasure hoard underground on the island you found me on in my jeweled ornament form for about one hundred and fifty years. That's enough inquiries for now. Your old home is odd. Everything that moves is so . . . It's nothing like this world."

"It's an ineffable shock speaking to someone that isn't Jaow-kieen. It's been too long. I . . ." I trailed off.

"Same here," she gave me an empathetic pat on the back. The contact sent a rippling pulse through my fire-changing body. Immediately blue bolts of energy danced on my back while orange lava danced over An-u's finger. We observed this inexplicable occurrence in the brief moment that it took place.

"What was that all about?" she asked.

"I have no idea."

"Where are we walking to?" I asked after several minutes passed.

"I'm taking us to my father."

"You know where he is in this behemoth maze of endlessness?" I asked, beyond appalled.

"I don't know anything about this place, but he's predictable!"

In what seemed to be a little under two hours, she led me over countless bridges and I followed her as we climbed down several pillars. The hulking body of Jaow-kieen was peacefully asleep outside the entrance of the maze. His goliath wings covered all of him except his tail and snout. An-u sprinted over to him and leapt onto his snout, throwing her arms about him. Deep rumbling purrs slightly shook the ground.

"You have returned, Zammus, after a couple days. I would like to speak with Zammus in private, An-u. My little Azura flame, I am beyond delighted that you've decided to walk in your physical form again."

Days? That can't be. I shook my head dazed, as if trying to shake off a fog I hadn't even seen descend.

An-u happily rubbed her face against her father's nose again before climbing down.

"Come, Zammus," beckoned Jaow-kieen in a gentle tone as he rose onto his four mighty legs.

We both walked alongside each other for many moments.

"I am sorry, Zammus. I sincerely am. As your mentor and as an entity that cares about you, I need to better understand that, like us all, you have limits. I will do all I can to be much greater at the effectiveness of understanding you and knowing when to give you a rest period. I've always been so hard on myself even before Maldroto came down. Billions or more years of thinking like that doesn't at all help preserve the positive qualities of the spirit that are so mandatory in nurturing, cultivating, and inspiring the psychology of others when it comes to the regards of strength and other benevolent virtues. You'll see a better change in me. One centered around heavy compassion," spoke Jaow-kieen candidly.

Though I was filled with anger, hostility, and degrees of animosity, I felt such negative and useless emotions flow away and leave. Such feelings would do nothing for the present or future circumstances to come.

"I appreciate your sincere apology and I accept your kind reflections. If we are to have a successful and beneficial relationship as mentor to student and friend to friend, then we will need to better understand each other's emotions. This will take time to adapt to and perfect. I'm willing to undergo this transformation so I can execute my duty. Let's start training from where we left off, Jaow-kieen," I answered.

Jaow-kieen nodded, "Let us go back to An-u," he said.

5

Cerebrations

"You will meditate three times a day. At dawn when you wake, at midday, and in the evening before you rest," spoke Jaow-kieen.

"Meditation?" I asked.

"Yes, the mind is the strongest link where all the four strengths–spiritual, mental, emotional and physical–draw from. I should have begun training your mind and body in synergy since the beginning. Throughout the day, aside from cultivating your inner strength, I shall tax and drain your physical. Now we will have a balance and hopefully necessary fruitful results."

"Okay," I shrugged in acceptance, not having a choice.

"Isolate yourself in the maze. Find a place that your mind deems as tranquil and comfortable. Then enter your mind. Embrace the fact that you are going to be in there just as much or maybe even more than you are out here," he said moving his forepaw through the air.

"Let's do this," I said.

"I will wake you when its time."

"Bye, Zammus!" chirped An-u, reappearing from under her father's wings.

"Bye. See you and Jaow-kieen after."

I was in no man's land. I entered the limitless maze of stone columns and bridges. Seeking change through transformation, I was beyond horrified. *What would I find within my mind?*

I understood full well that rumination under these conditions would be incomparable to anything I had ever experienced before. I sat on a bridge that was a little over a meter from the ground and crossed my legs into the lotus position. I observed the five suns above, locked my eyes on a crack in a random piece of stone, and shut my eyes. I entered blackness and felt myself falling into the abyss of my mind. My body was infinitesimal; it was nothing. Explosions of unrestrained and feral thoughts broke free from their recesses and swallowed me. Memories flashing by in rapid succession, depictions of love: familial, friendly, intimate, the spasmodic happiness and pain, and misunderstanding associated with all the species and subspecies of love. These notions twisted into clear images of loss and desolation.

Cliffs rushed into my field of sight, black monstrous rocks with jagged edges and needle teeth. Impaled on the rocks were human corpses. The slivers pierced every aspect of the deceased. A man with pallid white skin lay belly up with shards protruding out of his abdomen. To his left lay a woman with a very dark ebon complexion. Her body was positioned in a state of shock. Her torso and face were staring up at the sky. Her dark cocoa features were contorted in utter horror and crazed agony. Four spears had pierced the underside of both her breasts, come out through the top of her bosom, and punctured her throat. Her mouth was wide open as she cried out in silence and where her eyes should have been were gaping black holes.

The cliffs and environment around me melted into oily black ink. I ran and, having escaped my fears for the moment, I found myself in an empty lush green field with grass up to my knees. In front of me stood a white stone pedestal with a black thorny rose. I picked up the black flower . . . and I woke up.

"It's time," Jaow-kieen spoke from above me, bellowing hot air in my face. "Hop into my forepaw," he said flipping its underside toward the sky.

I complied. With a gentle burst of his wings we were airborne and rapidly moving across the maze. A black structure came into view. It was made up of horizontal and vertical poles that were fused together. Most curious were a pair of black loops, each suspended on a translucent rope-like cable that was somehow part of the horizontal bar supporting them. Jaow-kieen gently deposited me on the rocky platform that held the structure.

"You will master all of the body weight techniques associated with this apparatus. Make your way over to the goshii."

"The what?"

"The rings suspended on the ropes."

I reached for them and swung my body up. Instantly my arms and shoulder muscles screamed in pain.

"Time for the best part, my instruction!" grinned Jaow-kieen, revealing his brown-and-silver-stained teeth.

For the next several hours Jaow-kieen killed my arms, shoulders, chest, and back by having me alternate between overhand and underhand grips and holding my body in static positions for several seconds at a time.

"You may stop," he said kindly.

My muscles failed me and I fell. My mentor caught me in his paw.

"We are now going to a place that will rejuvenate you."

My eyes closed.

"Come on, Zammus," Jaow-kieen nudged me awake.

A red and orange lake filled all of my vision.

"This is the energy pool."

The dragon opened his paw and stood me up. And then I tumbled headfirst into the sea of lava. Crimson see-through bubbles erupted out of my mouth. *Hmmph,* I breathed. My limp body sunk deeper and deeper and deeper and deeper. My eyes suddenly burst open. My arms and legs violently struck out in all directions as fire and life flowed into my pores. Flaming strength and suppleness filled my being as I absorbed the lava. With renewed vigor I pushed my arms and legs widely apart as I started ascending to the surface. My torso erupted out of the lava and I swam over to Jaow-kieen. When I had waded out of the lava I became aware of this heaviness in my left shoulder. It was not painful or burdensome, just annoying, especially since I was currently stretching my arms.

I turned my head to the side and tilted it downwards to inspect my shoulder. *It's probably some sort of bite. Something most likely nipped at me when I was in the lava,* I thought absently. A smooth patch of gray rock or stone was sticking out of my deltoid, not far from my collar bone. Curiously intrigued, my fingers explored it. It was no bigger than my thumb and was triangularly-shaped. Puzzlingly there were no entry points or trauma to the region where it had pierced my flesh. Nor was there any pain, not even the slightest existing ache. Dartingly my eyes wandered to the rest of my shoulder. Around the wedge-shaped stone was a thin triangular layer of the same texture branching outward from the center an inch in each direction.

The layer of stone gradually thinned and then there was my teak-colored skin. The hairs slowly stood up all over my body and the highest on the back of my neck. The stone and my skin slowly and gradually differentiated from each other, like a dark tone of skin gently merging and transitioning towards a lighter shade on the same part of the body, the gradual transition from dark to light. Utterly horrified, I realized. This was no piece of stone sticking out of me. This piece of stone was growing out of me!

***

Later that evening Jaow-kieen and I were sitting in front of a huge blazing fire that the dragon had breathed into existence. I had meditated shortly after what Jaow-kieen called my fire bath.

"What do you think this is? How can it be here? Why?" I asked, feeling the rocky growth for the hundredth time.

"That's the twelfth time you asked me! And yes, I've been counting. I don't have all the answers, Zammus."

"What if?"

"Zammus, you are going to have to have to figure this one out on your own. Now please, enough about that! A dragon can only take so much!"

"Only so much?!" I laughed. "You've endured a billion and one things!"

"Well, actually a trillion and two! Oh, shut up!" laughed Jaow-kieen, gently slapping my back with the tip of his tail. With his right forepaw he slid something over. It was bowl-shaped.

"What is that?" I asked.

"Food." He uncovered the object with his paw and revealed a wide bowl that seemed to be made of rust and copper-colored clay. Liquid fire churned around in its depths.

"I am not consuming that!" I gawked, beyond appalled. "I can't! I don't have the body for it!" I reasonably protested.

"Yet you can swim in boiling lava and come out completely unscathed. Before, you didn't have the body you have now. Every species on Terra Draco eats this. This is all we need for nourishment. You are one with the fire now. One of the flame. One of us. Eat. If not, you'll starve."

I frowned into the bubbly orange and red liquid.

"Your body will physically reject anything else you feed it," mumbled Jaow-kieen, reading my mind.

With the utmost reluctance and donning the largest grimace imaginable, I dipped my hand into the lava bowl, scooped up the liquid, closed my eyes, brought it to my lips, and drank.

"Well?" Jaow-kieen grinned expectantly.

"Tastes like death," I said matter-of-factly.

"What would you know of death?" he asked.

"Well, I have died you know and still am dead you know, so . . ." I spoke sarcastically.

"Well, technically . . ." Jaow-kieen wandered off.

Paying him no mind, I took another mouthful of the glop. "Have you always eaten this stuff?" I moaned with disgust.

"That is all we creatures of flame have ever known."

Suddenly my thoughts grew dark and grim. "How strong is Maldroto, truly? How long until he escapes from his bonds?"

I stared into Jaow-kieen's fire-lit face. His red and golden scales were calm. They were small and triangular towards his snout and wide angular jaw. From there the scales grew into wide rippling circles. His multitude of horns were truly menacing. Six outward curving tusks grew from each cheek. An array of at least a dozen spikes adorned the crown of his head. They made him look beyond savage and wicked. The ridge of spines that went down the length of his spine and ended at the tip of his tail began on his head and neatly divided the rows of his cranial horns. His nostrils were oval-shaped and looked wide enough to fit a rhinoceros or elephant at most. The dragon's stark golden eyes were troubled and his deep pensive slits suggested that he was looking through the past.

"Alone he has enough power to obliterate a handful of worlds. With an army, enough strength and force to wipe out and rebuild existence," Jaow-kieen breathed.

"NO! How can that be?! And if that were true, then how could Terra Draco have prevailed and stopped him?"

"We didn't stop or defeat him. We subdued him. And it took more lives than the amount of stars my daughter and I traveled to find you."

"How is that–how can that even be possible?" I asked, my mouth wide enough to fit a pumpkin.

"Oh, but it is. According to his most faithful spies, sycophants, and warriors that were captured and tortured to reveal the truth about him, we learned that Maldroto was the spawn of ten or so different godly forces at once."

I gulped, hiccuped, and began to sweat profusely all at once.

"Our lone salvation and reason for still being, the Anuras were utterly godlike in power. We, myself included, made them from the strongest forces of this planet: the raw Life Krystals that grow in the central heart of the planet. One of these gems, Zammus, have the power to grant a lifeform endless life and immunity to anything–well, almost anything. The Anuras were made from dozens of them."

"Were they alive?" I asked fearfully.

"No. They have the life of a rock. Life like An-u can be made from them. But these krystals do not come from life themselves."

"Why are they called Life Krystals? Is it due to them advancing and eventually optimizing the life force of a living entity and being able to sustain them through infinite strength for eternity? Quite literally?" I queried.

"Yes. An-u was made from several thousand, five to be exact."

"Does she know how powerful she is?"

"No. Please promise me that you will not treat her differently because of that," announced Jaow-kieen.

"I promise," I replied, sincere and looking into his eyes.

"You asked about time earlier. It will take five centuries for Maldroto's bonds to be weak enough for him to break free. Well, close to six actually."

"So what does that mean for us three?"

"We'll be in this spirit bubble for five hundred years exactly. Training."

I was silent. What could I say? Processing this wasn't possible. I just tried to remain silent and calm.

"Are there any more Life Krystals left in existence?" I asked.

"No, not in the spirit world or the physical."

"Enough about that," Jaow-kieen's fearsome jaws snapped.

"We leave this place before dawn," he spread his wings open.

"What?!"

"Good night, Zammus." The dragon's wings erupted around him like bursting tidal waves and he shot into the night, his silhouette gliding against the stark aqua moon. I was beyond uneasy.

What was this trip thing all about? Why would Jaow-kieen wait until the last moment to tell me? We had been joking and sharing a pleasant moment. And now this! I sighed in ardent frustration. *You had to ruin it, didn't you. Bringing up Maldroto and all.* I groaned, cursing myself. I curled up in front of the flames and allowed the sprightly embers to flicker and dance before my eyes. They narrowed as the weight of the day collapsed on my chest. Through closed lids I traveled to realms beyond. A scorched landscape scarred by orange veins of lava engulfed my vision. A volcano belching smoke towered through the soot clouded air.

A dusty ball that had to be the size of a melon rolled into existence. The sphere came to a halt and opened. Four little legs and a sharp head and tail plopped into view.

"An armadillo!" I exclaimed pleasantly surprised.

The cute animal bounded over to me and wrapped its underbelly around my ankle. I swooshed it into my arms and brought it close to my face. Eagerly expressing its thanks, it licked me. Laughter leapt out from my lungs. The armadillo squealed in joy.

"Zammus! Zammus! Zammus! Zam-mus!"

I jolted awake to the sight of Jaow-kieen's golden yellow eye inches from my own.

"We're going. An-u is coming with us. Get your staff."

"I don't know where it is. It's lost in this maze somewhere. An-u came out of it."

Jaow-kieen growled out something. Less than a moment later the azure rod was seen gliding through the air, sailing towards me. Within seconds the sapphire staff was in my hand.

"Magic! Sorcery! How did you?" My mouth fell open.

"Later. Do know that us dragons are not just masters of science," smirked Jaow-kieen. "Climb up," he said tapping his great paw on the ground. I climbed onto it and scaled up his arm, onto the boulder of his shoulder. Gently easing myself onto the scaly ridges, I squeaked as my sensitive places made contact with sharp scales.

"Jaow-kieen, we have a bit of a problem!" I yelled.

"What?" he sighed impatiently.

"I am not 'designed' to ride on the backs of dragons without, ummm, . . . protection. I could get, ummm, . . . pierced and cut up down there if you know what I mean!" I growled in embarrassment and discomfort.

"An-u will help tend to your predicament," he replied.

"What?" I panicked, sweating like a carrot being steamed.

"What?" A voice protested not far behind me.

"We don't have time for this!" Jaow-kieen barked.

"Fine," An-u gritted her teeth.

I didn't even know she was up here! I thought as my cheeks burned uncomfortably hot.

I heard An-u move her arms and in an even voice she said these words:

"Ash Ârí zelsus!"

Suddenly my posterior and inner thighs were being enveloped by a cool liquid-like material. I flinched again as the material squeezed my inner thighs. I looked down and saw a pair of shorts that ended just at mid-thigh. They were form fitted and brown. Most impressive was the outer layer of armored brown rock that protected my outer and inner thighs and most importantly my delicates.

Turning to An-u, I thanked her.

"You look very strange."

"Does no one on this planet wear any clothes?" I asked incredulously.

"Clothes?" wondered An-u.

"Let's go!" yelled Jaow-kieen.

And with that he opened his mountainous wings and with furious wing strokes tore through the air.

"Where are we going?" An-u asked me.

"Not the slightest clue. He just told me about this last night. And he rushed!"

"He always has a reason for everything he does. Hopefully we both find out soon!" She smiled at me. Her shiny glass-like features fascinated me.

Jaow-kieen was well over the maze. From here I was able to make out that it was a dark brown square that extended in all directions that even from this height I could not entirely see.

"Goshii Oüshîn Wutâ iesin Shâtá!" Jaow-kieen commanded.

A chunk of maze broke from the rest in a violent explosion of bursting rock that raced through the air towards us.

"JAOW-KIEEN!" I cried.

"No worries," An-u shrugged.

"Shusara vílm rö vâ Dräk!" Jaow-kieen bellowed.

Whatever chunk of maze would have been visible contorted and folded in on itself, loudly crashing and grinding together before shrinking out of sight.

"Why didn't you tell me you were a sorcerer, Jaow-kieen? And An-u too?" I laughed, shocked.

"It's never fun knowing everything now, is it?" Jaow-kieen chuckled.

"I suppose not!" I called.

Suddenly An-u's fingers were on my shoulder. Her fingers, despite their hard krystal texture, were actually warm.

"What is that?" she gently tapped the rock on the side of my shoulder. I turned my head and looked at her sapphire frown.

"I don't know," I said, peering sideways.

"Was it like this yesterday?" she asked.

"Like what?"

"Did it cover your entire shoulder blade?" An-u ventured.

"No," I said in a quiet voice as my blood froze like ice over the Atlantic.

Shortly after our conversation a cold wind washed over all three of us. A black droplet landed on my hand. Two more fell and then an entire sea of black unloaded on us. Jaow-kieen roared out a swear. An-u moved up and sat alongside me.

"Bluribula Ingulftias," the words left her mouth and I could have sworn that I saw emerald sparks flash on her lips. In a split second the green fire was gone. In that same instant an emerald bubble had engulfed Jaow-kieen, shielding us from the elements. I inclined my head to An-u in gratitude.

"An-u, my dear, I appreciate this, but it's not safe. Not now. We have enemies out here and this will–"

Whatever Jaow-kieen was going to say was cut off as something large and round hammered his head. At that same moment white blade-like wings sliced through An-u's shield of light. The sorcerous bubble burst into fragmented shards. Jaow-kieen's limp body dipped forward and the attacker's wings swiveled and launched me off of Jaow-kieen. And into the open sky.

"JAOOOW-KIIIEEEEN!"

"ANNNN-UUUU!"

"FATTHERRR!"

"FATTHERRR! WAKE UP! WAKE UP! PLEASE! PLEASE WAKE UP! FATHER!" An-u wailed.

"ANNNN-UUUUU!" I cried hopelessly.

"ZAMMUS!"

And then I was too far to have been heard or hear. Three enormous dragons were carrying Jaow-kieen's body and roaring in victory.

"We've been so lucky to find you. Had that green charm never been fixed we'd have never found you!" one cackled.

"Our master's been wanting the Great, the Brave Jaow-kieen since you locked him up!" another snorted.

"Now our master can finally feed. You will give much strength to our master. Maldroto shall finally rise again!" a third voice intoned.

"HAIL MALDROTO!" chorused the three beasts.

Flailing hopelessly in the air, I felt as if I had been crushed underneath a ship and dragged through razor sharp coral reefs.

"What am I going to do? And how?" I whispered despondently.

My back struck something, black doors opened and every conscious thought I had was lost.

6

Immeasurable Depth

I awoke. In a cell. Lying down on a flat slab of stone. Around me were bars of layered stone and krystal that encased my surroundings into a sphere of limited space. *Circular prison cells! How did I get here!?* My thoughts were racing. *Every time I black out I literally wake up in a different reality,* my mind sighed. *Frankly it's getting old and becoming exhausting.*

"Where am I?! What is this place?!" I called out.

"Rudda-Rark Prison Stronghold. The biggest collection of rapists, murderers, genocide leaders, cannibals, and the rest of the lot," a voice answered.

The lava in my veins stopped flowing. The complete utter darkness as well as this new piece of information was forcing my heart to hammer into my ears. Any faster and it'd explode!

"This impossibly fortified container is big enough to hold all the blood spillers of the spirit world," the same voice came again.

I silently gulped. "What are you here for?" I asked.

The speaker came forward and revealed itself to be a monstrous humanoid lizard, a prugala. It was at least a good foot and a half taller than me and had four to five times as much muscle mass and density.

"How can I see him in the dark?" I whispered inaudibly.

"A prugala said something unkindly to me. So I ripped out his intestines and strangled him with them. All with these," the prugala proudly displayed the knife-length claws that grew on his fingers. "What 'bout you?"

"I can't remember. I've killed way too many," I said smartly.

"Ahhh, you're one of those. I'm Azerock," he nodded at me.

"The name's Varden," I hastily lied. "Has anyone ever escaped?"

"Only once and that was ten thousand years ago, from what I've been told. Before any of the current inmates were even here. I've been here for three centuries. I'm never leaving here. No one ever is," Azerock sighed hopelessly.

"Oh," I mumbled, crestfallen.

Azerock withdrew far into his cell and out of sight. I lay back on the rock bed and rested my head on my arms. There weren't any pillows here.

I need to rescue Jaow-kieen and An-u! I have to! I thought furiously.

My mind turned back to what Jaow-kieen's dragon captors had said about Maldroto. And I deeply wondered, *How can he have power in this spiritual realm? How much strength is he amassing before he gains enough to return to the physical world? How much time do I truly have to save the lives of Jaow-kieen and An-u? How much time until Maldroto's power grows and allows him to move on into the physical world? And how am I supposed to stop him?*

"I can't do anything for anyone until I am out of here. Focus on the present. Formulate a way to get out of here and go from there. Have a plan," I whispered to myself.

The explosive bombarding noise of goliath grinding stone gears and immense krystal chains being pulled taut shook the entire prison down to its clay foundation. Enormous cogs and pulleys rattled and whined as my eyes watched a ceiling disc that had to span several acres across be painstakingly slid to the right. With a thud that felt and sounded like a colossal earthquake, the disc stopped moving and the ancient machinery ceased their laboring. Through the opening in the prison's ceiling shone blazing white sunlight. In unison millions of prisoners retreated and cowered from its penetrating rays. Of the few who didn't flinch before its heavenly presence were Azerock and I.

From the suns' illumination I was able to see that my neighbor was crisscrossed from head to thigh in a tattoo of vicious scars. Looking all around me, I saw a diversity of species in orb-shaped cells of various sizes: sandfoots, basilisks, prugalas, and, yes, even dragons. All of them confined in giant globular cages that were arranged horizontally and vertically in countless rows that extended into infinity. All of them put here to literally live through eternity. Azerock flicked his emerald-yellow eyes onto me.

He can see what I'm not! Not any one of these creatures in the cells! My heart dropped to my feet.

Azerock's black pupils were wide and fully dilated. They swirled in amazement, shock, confusion, and rage, then blazed to utter hatred.

"NAWGA!" he spat, gritting his dagger-shaped teeth and launching a green glob of mucus from his chest and into my cage. There was a momentary silence as every beast with a scale eyed me. With unrestrained aggression they flung themselves in my direction, battering themselves against their krystal barred cages. Roars, growls and vocalizations of pure hatred pierced me.

"Excrement breather!"

"Feces dweller!"

Bile, bodily waste, and all sorts of fluids were flung in my direction.

"Cherish and savor this, demon!" a voice barked from above as something warm and clumpy splattered over my shoulder blades. Not shortly after I felt a hot stream of liquid being ejected onto my back.

"I'll shove my horn up your hole and impale you on my tusks, you scaleless wretch!" another voice hollered.

Feces and worse things covered me from head to toe. I painfully closed my eyes as more substances hit me in the face. I lowered my head, hunched down until my posterior could almost touch my ankles, and wrapped my arms around myself. And that's how I stayed bundled into a tight piteous ball as the endless tumult of curses, insults, and inhumane defilement pummeled me. Droppings were not the only things running down my hidden face. My broken soul was streaming from my eyes and gushing down my cheeks in endless waves.

***

An unknown amount of time passed. Maybe six or seven suns and moons had shined down my back. I couldn't be sure though, since I never looked up out of fear of having something horrible fall into my eyes. The ever-present warmth on my back could have either been two things: the suns' rays or fresh bodily waste. My senses had long deadened to the incomprehensible stench. One day, to my endless horror, all the cages around me clicked open. Bodies bounced into my cage. Claws tightened around my arms, piercing and slicing into my tissue. I screwed my eyes shut even tighter. The front of my feet scraped against a stone floor as I was dragged.

Where and by who? Guards, enemies, who knew? I didn't care. Not anymore. I was brutally flung onto the floor in a heap, landing on my back.

"Open your eyes, NAWGA!" a voice hissed by my ear.

"Why? Does it matter?" I whispered.

"Open your eyes you insolent, arrogant wretch or I'll tear your eyelids off!" another voice spat into my other ear.

With exhaustion I squinted my eyes open. One four-armed basilisk, two prugalas, a sandfoot, and a small dragon the size of a carriage surrounded me. I regarded them all with apathy. With a graceful leap the serpent wheeled like a loop through the air and brought the hardened segmented scales on the tip of its flexed, currently U-shaped tail down onto my abdomen with enough force to completely deflate my stomach, burst the air out of my lungs, slam my head wickedly against the floor, and draw a gush of lava out of my throat. The serpent pressed me deeper into the floor as it bounced off of me and leapt into the air to hammer and slam my body again.

I winced as its lithe body came crashing down . . .

Suddenly something blue flashed and buried itself in the serpent's skull, coming out the back and killing it instantly. The body struck a nearby wall and crumpled to the floor. Everyone, including myself, blinked in shock and confusion. The corpse jerked upward a little as the blue shape yanked itself out with a *squelch!* A familiar sapphire krystal rod hovered in the air.

"My staff," I whispered inaudibly.

The blue rod tilted in my direction, as if to acknowledge me.

"Enough of these tricks!" charged the sandfoot, thundering forward, rearing its three bull-like horns. In less than a second the staff whipped around, dived through the air, and struck the beast on one of its ten legs with enough force to break the limb and have it laying belly up on its shell. With a decisive flick, it struck it on its head. It lay still, breathing, yet subdued. The dragon and two prugalas were fleeing the scene. In a spinning blur the staff struck them all on their heads and like their friend they were all swallowed by the gaping jaws of unconsciousness.

"Thank you ever so much," I breathed.

How did it find me? The staff still in midair, swiveled forward, suggesting that I follow it. It came to rest at the level of my hand and waited.

"Oh!" I chirped after a couple of seconds, closing my fingers around its shaft. Wasting no time to steady itself it raced forward at an incomprehensible speed, barely giving me the chance to wrap my other hand around it. We zipped through various halls and passageways. Several times the instrument of my salvation would suddenly jerk left or right, soar up drastically, or swoop down alarmingly. All I could do was further tighten my grip and rattle my teeth.

"I can't believe you're busting me out!" I struggled to say through a mouthful of air. We zipped past a confused dragon that was on guard. By now the halls were pulsing with an uproar of shouts, the most common being, "The nawga is missing! It's escaping! Secure the perimeter!"

The staff twisted in another turn. We were racing towards another brown wall. And approaching at breakneck speed.

"Aren't you going to turn?" I yelped.

The staff increased its velocity. I was dozens of yards from becoming a splat on the wall! With a throbbing vibration it changed its shape into a heavily thickened shield battering ram, extending over my head and body in a star-shaped casing. From my elbows down I was protected by layer after layer of krystal.

"OH NO! OH NO! NO! NO!" I hollered, realizing that we were going to hit the wall. "It has to be at least three to four feet thick! I'm going to die! I can't do this! We won't make it! I'm going to die! I'm going to die! Again!" I cried.

With an incredibly frightening and painful bone juddering sensation and a titanic eruption of rock and masonry, we were out of Rudda-Rark Prison Stronghold. The vigorous afternoon suns raged through my vision. Three were spread out in a linear blade high in the heavens. The other two were arranged on either side of the sun that either formed the beginning or end of the solar line segment. *Looks like a sword,* I thought. The three blazing spheres, one in front of the other formed the blade and the two on the end formed the hilt.

"Hey, I's spotted the demon! Catch it! And kills it!" Voices returned me from my reverie and to present circumstances.

"Dragon guards: advance and pursue! Terminate and return most of the remains for 'generic' identification. Go! Go! Go!"

The staff, still engulfed in layers of krystal, propelled me forward and skyward. Tilting my head back, to my horror I witnessed the dragons, bear-sized brutes . . . *fwirling*. That was the only way I could think to describe it, they were reappearing in flashes of bright light in the space I'd occupied but a moment ago. Several hundred meters above the prison and hiding in the glare of the suns, I sighed in relief as I watched the guards hovering, squinting, and staring in open befuddlement. For five to seven minutes their search endured until the lot of twenty dolefully slumped their wings and shuffled back into the gaping breach in the wall.

Only one sentry remained and his gaze was frozen on where I lay hiding. For the longest time the guard looked at where I was.

He can't possibly see me! His eyes can't penetrate the blinding glare of five suns. True enough, the guard lowered his gaze and quickly darted back into the hole in the penitentiary's framework. Just two grateful gulps of air later, the same guard returned with a troop of ten behind him. I choked as my gaze fell to what they were all wielding in their forepaws. Sledgehammers. The sapphire casing shielding my body accelerated away just as the eleven dragon guards materialized around us in bright bursts of dancing light. The krystal barrel holding me shot forward and a coat of spines grew over its surface. The dragons fwirled into view. My protector impaled three right through their bodies on a pike-length protrusion.

As the weapon withdrew back into krystal essence and the bodies fell, a guard struck just by my head with her hammer. In a stomach tossing maneuver the krystal flipped back and struck my assailant on her helmet. She sailed downward. Still being rushed forward by the powers of the staff, I noticed towering orange canyon walls looming before us on either side of my vision. A guard flung itself on the front of my azure carrier. Ramming itself forward with sorcerous speed, the vessel flung itself into the cliff wall, using the flesh of our assailant to completely protect itself. The guard's body broke with a sound that mirrored smashing bricks.

"We need to lose the remaining six. Not kill!" I said. "No more deaths," I ordered, not sure if it'd understand or even listen.

The sapphire blazed downward, zipping between columns of rock. The dragons clung right behind our tail.

"How do we lose them?!" I cursed.

However way we went, whether it was a swoop, curve, spin or roundabout, these guards would materialize.

"Go lower! Almost graze that sand below," I instructed. "We'll lose them in those sandbanks. It's our only chance!"

We dipped until the grains were just a hand's breath from touch. To the right lay a curving wall of stone that reached into the sky.

"If we go behind that wall at blistering speed, that'll give us a two second advantage. It'll take the dragons one second to fwirl and another just to travel and close the distance between us. The second we dive below the sand we have to keep diving under it and moving through it. They could never find us through this ocean of sand. No one ever could!" I explained.

The wall closed in on us. I looked back. Our pursuers were just a yard away.

"NOW!"

The sapphire transport burst forward and whirled behind the lip of rock. My peripheral vision saw the six dragons disappear in flashes before the rock closed off my vision. *We got a split second!* I panicked.

"Dive! Now!" I roared.

Sand engulfed us like water at the speed we were going at. And from there we vanished from the surface world.

"Dive! Keep going! Keep going. Keep going. Keep going. Keep going. Keep going," I lazily repeated, even though it was no longer necessary. Nothing was behind us but worlds of sand. We glided through these sandy depths for I don't know how long. Was it an hour? Two? Three? Six? Who knew? The ever-present blue light lit up the continuous tunnels of sand that we were both making and instantly collapsing as we moved through the depths. One moment we were in sand and the next the krystal casing softly struck stone. We were positioned before the lip of a small chasm. I nodded.

"Deeper is better," I announced.

The krystal tipped us forward and we tumbled into a channel of lava that rushed us downwards and sideways with amazing speed as we moved with the magma swell. About five minutes later, we were deposited into a cavern that was both taller and wider than a cathedral. My krystal companion, who had ever so faithfully shielded me in a warm container, fought for, and protected me ceaselessly, shrunk down into its normal staff form in complete and utter exhaustion.

"Oh, thank you, my most valuable friend! My immeasurable gratitude for your most golden and epic deeds today cannot be expressed through mere words. I here from this day forward pledge to you my limitless faithfulness. This I swear to you, friend, as Zammus Dre' Suel!" I bent forward on one knee and dipped my head in inclination to the staff.

The staff rolled towards me as if to express its humble acknowledgment of my words. I saw that we were in a tunnel that extended and curved on both sides without end.

"Sleep well, my friend. You deserve it, more than anyone. May you recover your strength," I wished the staff.

I lay on my back, eying the lava flowing all over the walls. I felt the staff leap into my hand. It shrunk until its end rested against my forearm and comfortably nestled warmly into my palm. Through closed eyes I smiled and sleep took over.

7

Grains Of Wind

"Father! Zammus! Where are you?!" screeched An-u, ramming her fist into the wall. The stone brickwork groaned as it was forced into a small depression. In a moment or two the flaw in the wall cracked, pushed outward, and repaired itself.

"AAHHH!" An-u howled. That was the fifth time that her damage had been erased. The black walls that surrounded her on all four sides rose above her and loomed into eternity.

"I don't know how I got here or how long it's been since that horrible day that I lost them, but I need to get out of this pit I've been left to die in," she said. "But how?"

"Think, think, think!" she hummed, pressing her knuckles to her temples. There was utter darkness all around her, save the faint sapphire light that was gently pulsing from her body. She slumped back against the wall and sat down. She shivered as a breeze eased down from the wall and glided over her krystal skin, engulfing her arms. Though her mind was harboring hatred for everything at the moment, she did have an infinitesimal portion of gratitude for one thing: the cloak she had found when she first awoke here. Tucking her knees to her chest, she slithered deeper into the cloak and covered her head just as a colder wind ferociously gathered her in its arms.

***

"Arabula Moêr!" she whispered. To no surprise this spell, like all the other ones she had cast, failed to work. The howling winds from the previous night hadn't allowed her much rest and regardless how many times she wrapped the cloak about herself, the blade of the wind sliced right through it, parting it open again and again. She looked at her surroundings. A wide rectangular space of black stone, a glossy obsidian black just like the walls enclosing her. The space was barren with the exception of a white stone chair with spiraling designs coiling around its three spindly legs.

Aquamarine sunlight bleeding its rays gave her these details. An-u flexed her large muscular calves in frustration and stood up. The fluid in her stomach frothed and moaned hungrily. She walked to the nearest wall and, tracing her fingers along its sleek surface, felt for crags and handholds.

"None," she sighed.

Her swift investigation of the remaining walls confirmed nothing new. She hunkered down onto her bottom and stared at the white sand that was covering her blue toes. The same sand that was spread throughout the pit.

The sand! That's it! she thought, her mind racing.

"The sand could not have been dumped over the edge of this chasm. It had to have come from below! There has to be something beneath it," she whispered.

For several moments she weighed the option that she could be wrong and the sand would lead nowhere. But in the end the notion of doing nothing and not having a choice weighed greater. She looked up to see if there were any eyes watching. Without a second to lose, she thrust her palms into the sand and began digging.

8

Subterranean Social Pressures

I awoke with the staff in my hand. It pulsed with a warm effulgent turquoise hue.

"Hey," I grinned sleepily, rubbing my eyes to shake off the drowsiness. My companion shimmered and lengthened into a sleek sword. I got to my feet and looked about myself. With the sword in my hand I began to make my way down the behemoth tunnel. My eyes traced its magnificence; the walls could have held six dozen elephants had they been abreast. The height would have paralleled a cathedral. I was easing around a very wide bend. Sweat was cascading down my features.

Anything could be hiding up ahead and you'd never see it! My mind quivered as I trembled.

"There won't be anything behind the bend. There won't be a soul waiting to slay me! I swear!" I sung.

"There won't be anything behind the bend. There won't be a soul waiting to slay me! I swear! There won't be anything behind the bend. There won't be a soul waiting to slay me! I swear! There won't be anything behind the bend. There won't be a soul waiting to slay me! I swear!" I chorused.

My heart was leaping like a kangaroo as I made my way around the edge of the bend. Seeing nothing, I sighed like a hurricane. I proceeded with ease, exhaling assured breaths just like a blizzard.

"Ahhhh, so there you are! You thief!" bellowed a voice.

"HHHH!" I whipped around. "Where are you?!" I hollered, almost slipping.

A bellowing laugh that could have come from the throat and voice of God filled the cavern. My legs buckled and I fell.

"Look up, child," the Omnipotence softly commanded.

Slowly and steadily my head panned upwards. My heart almost lunged itself out of my stomach. A glowing green dragon that could have been Jaow-kieen's father, or his grand-father, or even his great grand-father was considering me. The length and girth of his body, which was upside down, was impossibly squeezed onto the ceiling, only small gray and white gaps of it were visible. Golden energy was glittering and dancing all over his body. White stars of light were flickering on every one of his lime green scales.

"What are you? Who are you?" I squeaked.

With a titanic heave, the dragon flipped itself off the ceiling and onto the floor, dexterously landing on all fours. The ground I was standing on violently rose up into a maze of wedged cracks. The streams of lava that hugged the walls in cascading flows danced off the stone in eruptions of chaos.

He opened his jaws and my entire body vibrated. "I am Vaughn-ness, the very first dragon and the creator of their race. You have been causing a swirling mountain of trouble. And so has your friend," he flicked a purple tongue towards the staff, which had shrunk into a hand-sized ball.

"How could you possibly know this?" I shivered.

Padding softly, Vaughn-ness approached me, stopping when his snout was an arm's length above me.

"You are curious," he said.

Great jets of air shot up the caves of his flaring nostrils.

"You smell of dragon. Just like me and all my children. Yet you are . . . not . . . you have not a single scale to your name, yet you have pure dragon essence about you–and something else. Something ancient, that predates Maldroto's arrival, and even my time. Even the time of . . . dragons."

"What do you mean? What are you saying? How can any of this make sense?" I gasped, overwhelmed.

"Who are you? What are you, boy? And most importantly how did you come about this place? Tell me!" roared the colossus.

"I–I–I . . ."

"Yes," Vaughn-ness growled. The claws closest to me dug into the stone, crunching it into fractures as if it were parchment. I gulped, realizing my lack of a choice in telling the truth.

"I was being chased by dragon guards and my friend here was protecting me. It got to the point where our pursuers had us cornered in a canyon flooded with sand. We lost them by diving into the sand. From then on the staff led us into these cavernous tunnels. We rested for the night and awoke fresh this morning, with no choice but to explore and see where they led to. And then I spotted you on the ceiling. You asked me who and what I am. I can only answer one of your questions. I am Zammus Dre' Suel, former marine navigator of the ship, the *Mantis.* As for what I am, I no longer know anymore."

"What were you before? What did you used to be?"

Vaughn-ness asked in a soothing and gentle voice.

"Human. A human being. I was part of humankind. I didn't have this magma lava in my veins or this rock growing out of me!"

Vaughn-ness solemnly angled his neck, drooping his oval-shaped head in empathy.

"Let it out, Zammus Dre' Suel," he encouraged.

"What?! How on earth could you say that? I'd never expect . . ."

"Continue to let it out. Express all that anger, rage, sorrow, grief, pain and confusion."

"I–I–I–I don't know what to say."

Huge soft violet-bluish eyes pored over me.

"Maybe you don't have to say. Maybe you should express through action. Break something. Make something. Catharsis. The eternal ember of the soul."

I looked at my shoulder, the one with the wedge of stone. The gray fragment now engulfed the entire front and lateral part of it and small gravel-sized grains were homogenizing themselves onto the strip where my bicep and shoulder fused. I tapped my stone deltoid.

"Do you have a cure for this, Vaughn-ness?"

His head shook from side to side, "I'm afraid not."

Tears flooded from the dams of my eyes.

"There, there," he said, wrapping a titanic grass-green wing over me.

"Can you at least tell me what's happening to me?" I snuffled.

The elder's warm eyes changed to a glowing yellow. When they were back to violet-blue, his tone was grave, "It will be painful."

"I've known nothing, but pain. Endless pain. Please, tell me. I deserve to know."

"Are you sure?" he warned, squeezing the circular scales under his eyes in a look of pain.

"Yes."

The plated scales on Vaughn-ness's chest puffed outward as he took a long deep breath. My sapphire companion suddenly rippled and split into two parts. A wide, dome-shaped shield and a pike shaft appeared in both my hands, painting the walls an azure blue with their sorcerous energy.

"Danger!" I warned.

The scales covering Vaughn-ness stood up on end, giving him a very spiky and savage appearance. A hill-sized shadow was looming around the bend that I had appeared from. Vaughn-ness stepped forward and my weapons thrummed. A white-and-brown striped dragon with animated orange eyes entered the tunnel.

"Hi, I'm Yvylara. If I remembered right, Zammus, is it?"

"How do you know that name?" I retorted, still not lowering my spear.

"Dar Vagoue, he was poisoned, remember?"

DAR! My mind gasped as memories flushed through my consciousness. Our initial encounter in front of the blazing green fire in the mudlands, the battle with the magma centipedes where he received a terribly venomous bite, the story he told me about his life while I cradled him in my paw in dragon form on the flight to Euphasoü so he could get treatment that would save his life, the arrival to Euphasoü, and the dragon who stole him from my care and that I had flown after. My mind was blank, from that point on Jaow-kieen was in the picture.

You stole him, Yvylara! You stole Dar's weak and sickened body from me, slightly vexed, I furrowed my brow as I connected the dots.

"How do you know this?" I said, strategically measuring my response. *For now, the less she knows the better,* I thought.

A burst of white air left the female dragon's snout.

"Dar Vagoue insisted that I find you. A couple weeks after your bizarre death–yes, I witnessed it, it was in my cave–I sought a sorcerer who'd let me into the spirit world for a period of ten years."

"How long has it been since you were granted entry into this realm?" I asked.

"Eight years, going on nine."

I've been dead for eight years! My brain flipped in my head. I felt unsteady as if her words had been a blizzard of knives made of ice.

"Why should I trust you? How do I know you aren't false?" I asked logically.

"I knew that you'd eventually reach that conclusion, my friend," a voice pronounced evenly.

A shadow was travelling down the wall of the bend. A dark brown-and-green scaled prugala with a giant semicircular scar that stretched across his chest, down his ribs, and ended at his waist appeared.

"That's why I came. It was the only way to convince you," he grinned broadly, showing a bottom and top row of small sharp teeth.

"DAR VAGOUE! YOU'RE HEALED!" I held out my arm to him. He gripped it.

"All thanks to him," he pointed to another figure that entered the tunnel.

It was a dragon that had deep orange scales with a small portion of brown stripes. He was more or less the same size as Yvylara. I looked over at Vaughn-ness for the first time since Yvylara had arrived. His scales were lowered a little bit and he transferred his bemused expression to my eyes.

"Shárohlas, botanist, medical doctor and surgeon, experienced apothecary, herbalist, and healer at your service," the dragon arched its neck in my direction. For but a moment, my eyes wandered over to the various bags and satchels that were draped over and hanging from both sides of his body.

"Zammus at yours," I nodded back.

By now Vaughn-ness was at ease. The shield and spear in my hands flared warm in my palms and shifted into a baton, the length of my forearm.

"I just knew that I had to come and see you when my sister described your unknown anatomical transformation from a dragon's biology to the physiognomy you currently possess–"

"You can alter your shape into that of a dragon?" Vaughn-ness asked in a tone that suggested utter horror.

"Yes," I confirmed.

"–Not to mention I came here to protect my sister and Dar Vagoue," Shárohlas nodded to Yvylara.

"Ahmmmm," I murmured.

"Well, Zammus, we found you! Mission success and mission complete! We can go back to the world of the living now," Dar Vagoue smiled.

"I can't. I have lives to save."

Jaow-Kieen, my mentor. And An-u with her dark, piercing azure eyes, my thoughts breathed.

9

Taut

An-u buried her face in her hands, sighing in despair. "This sand leads nowhere," she lamented.

She looked at all the small holes around her that she had dug. Forlornly she eyed the dozens of holes, all of them only as deep as her shoulder. She gazed down at the hole that she just dug. Like all the other ones, there was a thick layer of dirty copper, the color of iron oxide rust, covering the base of the hole.

"What's this?" She leaned forward, squinting curiously as she looped her finger around a thin ring sticking out of the metal. It easily slid over her middle finger. She caressed it with her thumb, thinking. With absolute faith that this could be her salvation, she tugged with all her might. Once, twice, thrice, and with a *pop!* she was lying flat on her back.

Something was wedged tightly in her right hand. She flicked her gaze over it; lying clutched in her palm was a bow made entirely of clear white shining krystal wrapped in spiraling silver that swirled over the long arch that held the bow string.

"Wow. How long has this been here?" An-u breathed.

Rocking forward onto her knees, she reappeared over the hole.

"There has to be a quiver with arrows here, somewhere. Even one," she puffed, sifting her palms over the base of the hole.

"Nothing, how very strange," she sighed in confusion as she withdrew her prying hands.

"Why would there be this spectacular bow without any arrows to fire? How could that be?" she wondered aloud. Her fingers curled around the bow, her eyes absorbing its incandescent quality. She caressed the captivating otherworldly runes deeply etched into its elongated, curving surface, then set her fingers on the string, rubbing it between her thumb and forefinger. It was a long, sleek golden cord, possessing a form of essence that was the epitome of graceful leanness and supple durability.

Enveloping the golden string was a translucent fiber, as thick as two of An-u's fingers. Squeezing with her thumb and forefinger she gently pulled the string back. A sonorous note pierced the enclosure of her surroundings. A pulse of golden light appeared in her hand. The light wiggled, elongating into a shape. A scream leapt out of An-u's throat as she found herself squeezing a firm, glowing, golden white arrow. Her heart was quivering in her chest though it was not fear that possessed her limbs, but an anxiety that was rapidly growing beyond control.

Still kneeling and without knowing why, she aimed the arrow at the sky. Taking a deep breath, she pulled the string back to its limit and released the arrow. A howl of utter horror thundered out of her lungs as a loop of golden light constricted around her wrist, connecting her to the arrow through a faint, barely visible white string of streaming light. An-u's howl rose to a stabbing screech as her body left the ground, being launched into the air. Into the heavens or wherever the arrow was going, An-u was too. Below her the abyss of her prison shrunk. At last she was finally free.

10

A Pernicious Sickness

Jaow-kieen's head, shoulders, and entire body remained defiant despite his circumstances. The steel chains reinforced with krystal were studded with barbs; deep purple blood was oozing from his wings, legs and tail. But he did not acknowledge any of this.

"How do you like our new cages for fire drakes? The one you're in is an upgraded design from the originals from the last great world war," lectured the only free dragon in the room. From the purplish-green orb that engulfed his snout, Jaow-kieen could make out that the guard had scales that were an incredibly filthy brown color. Once again, the thought of making fire in the back of his throat struck Jaow-kieen's mind. This time he couldn't suppress it. Chemicals erupted in his stomach and molecular compounds clashed with such natural violence that a sphere of flames was conceived in his lava-composed lungs. The ball of flame grew as a jet of magma and air secreted from his heart and arterial walls launched it up his esophagus towards his throat. Jaow-kieen reflexively opened his mouth and flared his nostrils to their maximum.

The slashing waves of fire roared against the sorcerous barrier restricting them. In a brief flash of blue the orb imprisoning his snout and jaws squashed and crushed the flame, utterly nullifying his attempt.

"What would make another dragon obliterate the flame of his brother? What would cause a dragon to extinguish the fire that gave him life? How could you turn your back on the sacred venerable flame that gives this world and us all life? Where is your honor? What happened to the scales of your dignity?" Jaow-kieen beseeched. A mountain of sorrow was growing in his throat.

"Spare me your ancient prattle, elder!" the guard spat.

"You post-war specimens are a disgrace to dra-kin. You know nothing of war, death, or time. And you know even far less of yourself. Or what your countless ancestors had to die for and impossibly sacrifice for you to even be here and exist," Jaow-kieen pronounced with piteous scorn.

The scales of the brown dragon rose with hatred into spiny formations.

"SILENCE!"

"Inferior ignorants such as you will be incinerated for their treachery. With all the pride in the world, I would happily obliterate you, so you could be free of your shameless and miserably corrupted existence," Jaow-kieen announced with finality.

"E-E-E-ENOUGH!" the younger dragon erupted, throwing himself at Jaow-kieen, gray talons aimed at his throat.

"Aseroph! That's enough! We need him alive."

The brown feral dragon was frozen in midair, held by an invisible sorcerous current of air. A shape appeared, strolling out of the shadows. Its silhouette was definitely reptilian.

Jaow-kieen squinted to better consider it as it came into the light. It had two legs and was very tall, a physically impossible trait for bipedals. It had a thick long tail that ended with a sickly barb surrounded by a crown of shards. Its torso was robust and accentuated by two burly arms that each sported a row of villainous spikes that ran from wrist to tricep. Four grand wings extended from its back. Resting on its impressively thick neck was an oval head completely covered in spines. Two wicked spiraling horns curved down its skull. Its entire body was a deep obsidian black, all with the exception of its glowing purple eyes.

"Who are you? What are you?" Jaow-kieen asked.

"I am V'rossar. You are going to tell me everything I need to know regarding Zammus Dre' Suel," the creature spoke.

"And if I refuse?" growled Jaow-kieen.

"Well . . ." V'rossar strolled forward pulling a long black savage spike laden with spines from between his wings. He came close to Jaow-kieen, so close that his quill-covered face was gently pressing against the gauntlet of armor of Jaow-kieen's scales where his paw merged into his wrist.

V'rossar lovingly rubbed his head onto Jaow-kieen's wrist most tenderly, "If you refuse to tell me–" And he jammed his spike into Jaow-kieen who bellowed and violently roared, thrashing in torture as his captor twisted and skewered it into his wrist. "–then I'll do this. It's okay. Be calm. Don't wail and behave as such."

V'rossar cooed as he dug the curving spear beneath the walls of hardened scales, ligaments, tendon, muscle, flesh and bone. He gracefully turned the spike again, grinning with absolute relish as it squelched into the bone marrow. Jaow-kieen's roars ascended to a titanic level of volume, bringing rocky fragments from the roof of the chamber smashing down to the ground. The enchantments holding Jaow-kieen protected him. Wherever a piece of stone struck V'rossar it disintegrated. He cast a protective bubble around Aseroph. With a sigh and baneful wrench, he yanked the spike out of Jaow-kieen.

An omnipotent howl filled the cave as a sea of purple blood flooded out of him.

"Next time you cry that loud, I'll cut it off," hissed V'rossar.

He repositioned the spear, which was covered in scraps of purple flesh, but didn't thrust. "Now, tell me everything you know about Zammus Dre' Suel."

"Never," Jaow-kieen declared.

"Very well," purred V'rossar and he stabbed again. This time Jaow-kieen felt the spear come out the back of his forearm.

11

Induction By Fire; A Metamorphosis

"Who do you have to save? And what can we do to help?" chirped Dar Vagoue with an unmistakable air of eagerness.

The stone beneath my feet hummed, and I landed hard on my posterior as the ground quickly shifted between a liquid and solid state.

"What was that?" I grunted as I shakily stood to my feet. "Is everyone okay?" I called out.

"They can't hear you, Zammus," Vaughn-ness explained. "I have temporarily frozen their minds and awareness."

"Why?"

"There are things I have to tell you. About yourself. Things you need to see. Things I must show you," Vaughn-ness declared, beaming at me with godly intensity through his purplish azure eyes.

"I have no objection to anything you've said. I need answers. I need to know what's happening to me and how I'm supposed to fulfill my purpose and the tasks that follow. But what about them?" I jutted my chin at the three perfect statues of Dar Vagoue, Yvylara, and Shárohlas.

They looked just as they were when they had been moving several seconds ago.

"Can they see us in that state?" I asked, growing disturbed.

"No. Nor can they operate with any of their five senses," answered Vaughn-ness. "Do I have your permission to sorcerously transfer them to a safe place in the physical plane? If I do so, no spell or phenomena with the exception of death will be able to bring them back here. It'll be for their safety," spoke Vaughn-ness.

"Just as long as that immobility spell is removed when they go back and that you guarantee that they are safe from all harm," I said firmly.

"Of course," assured Vaughn-ness.

He gently blew a long trail of air from his nostrils onto the air surrounding Dar Vagoue, Yvylara, and Shárohlas. A bubble of emerald and golden energy enveloped them. It rippled and pulsed twelve times, each time adding a layer of energy to the bubble's volume.

"Those shield layers will render them immune and invisible to evil minds and prying eyes," Vaughn-ness confirmed.

"Thank you very much for securing their safety." I nodded, studying the brown and white stripes of Yvylara's scales, the orange and brown of her brother's, and the savage scar on Dar Vagoue's torso. I mentally preserved his stern yet wholly determined blind gaze.

"I'll be there with you all the way when we see them again," Vaughn-ness rumbled softly.

"Alright, very well. Do what you must, please," I said.

He growled softly and brought his forepaw onto the stone with enough force to make it rise up into small cliffs that engulfed his paw. An emerald light rose off his scales and released concentric ripples into the stone. Two gear-shaped discs of light the size of boulders appeared on either side of us. Slightly tilting his head upwards, he beckoned the orb containing Dar Vagoue, Yvylara and Shárohlas towards the disc to our left. Mountains covered in green krystal vegetation revealed themselves.

"I really am sorry for this. We'll see each other again soon," I said, not knowing if that was true.

Vaughn-ness nodded forward and the globe of light encasing them bobbed into alignment with the disc and fused into it. In a glistening of heat and rainbow-colored light, they were gone. Only one window of light remained, its surface shimmering into iridescent pools of light. Through it a desert landscape gleamed. Growing out of the beige, yellow sand were countless towers of clear white krystal. In the very far distance I could make out the brownish-red and gray silhouette of a vast walloping mountain.

"Are you ready?" Vaughn-ness kindly asked.

I gulped and nodded.

He wrapped an entire claw around me and springing with his hind legs propelled us into the disc of light. Sand exploded around us as we thudded into it. I was thrown from Vaughn-ness's grasp. I lay on my stomach breathing heavily. Whatever force had hurled me from him had decided to deposit me with my head turned sideways. My neck muscles were overly strained and screaming in pain.

It's a thousand times better than having a broken neck and getting sand shoved into your nose and throat, my thoughts groaned.

Nearby I heard Vaughn-ness shaking the sand out of his scales.

"What was that?" I moaned.

"A portal. A ripple through the fragment of reality. And you are now aware that you can transport matter from one point of reality to another," Vaughn-ness explained.

He plucked me up off the ground and stood me up with a claw.

"You'll need this," he spoke heavily, dispelling warm air from his jaws over my entire body. The air around me shimmered and alternated from gold to clear. I felt tremendously heavier all of a sudden. Looking down at my body I saw that it was covered in a grayish-brown stone armor. I touched my head and my fingers found an orb-shaped helmet. My fingers explored my neck and caressed the armored frills encasing it. From head to toe I was covered in sphere-shaped segments of rock. The gauntlets on my hands revealed that the only part of my body that was visible were my eyes, and only because a wide oval slit allowed them.

"Wow! Oh, my goodness!" I laughed, incredulous. "How am I supposed to even walk in this? And what's it even for?"

"You'll find out," Vaughn-ness replied, looking towards the shadow of the mountain.

"Where are we? Where is this?" I asked.

"East of the city of Drukbaen. More or less, we're in the outskirts. And that ominous mountain is the first of a chain of over a thousand. Welcome to the foot of the Ank Ken Rancorn Mountains," he breathed.

I quickly nodded as my forehead under the helm melted into sweat. "Where's my staff?!" I exploded as the claws of panic ferociously squeezed my heart.

"It is here, I have it."

I whipped around to face Vaughn-ness and looked into his grand face. The three main largest horns on his face, two jutting out on either side of his forehead and one between his eyes, were gleaming under the gaze of the suns. His purple sapphire eyes were soft. He brought his tail close to me and like an elephant's trunk it curiously felt about a thick, ever drooping, saggy roll of layered grass-green scales on the side of his stomach.

His tail lifted the sagging flesh to my utmost disgust and inserted itself between the plentitude of folds. More of his tail disappeared as it wedged itself deeper and then with a plopping noise it withdrew, tightly clutching the godly staff in its tentacular grasp.

"Oh, Vaughn-ness! Thank you!" I exclaimed, throwing my arms about the hill of his arm. Deep grumbles of mirth-filled laughter shook his body. The staff leapt towards me as Vaughn-ness unwound his tail and happily darted around me as I climbed down his forearm.

"I'm very happy to see you too," I said amiably.

The staff split in two halves and shimmered, flattening into two equally-sized and identically-thin twin blades. I felt the swords secure themselves between my shoulders.

"Stay close to me, Zammus," Vaughn-ness growled.

My eyes fiercely darted around. The sky and the sand dunes around us were utterly barren.

"There's nothing here," I said in confusion.

Vaughn-ness's tail tightly coiled around me and we left the ground in a blur as his wings tore the sand into dust. Below, right where we had just been, a colossal magma centipede erupted and roared, its heat pressing into me in waves.

"How did you? . . ." I said breathlessly. "Why are we really here?" I asked, the grim reality finally settling in.

"As I said, to find the truth."

"About what?"

"About you," Vaughn-ness replied.

***

Vaughn-ness's claws clacked as he landed on the mountain.

"Vaughn-ness?"

"Yes?" he answered.

"When we first met you had told me that you were the creator of dragons. Could you please tell me how that came to be?"

Vaughn-ness's armored chest compressed inward as warm air poured from his mouth.

"I will, yet not now," he said firmly. "It's not the time, plus we don't know who or what could be listening around here," he said in a softer tone.

"I can agree with that," I said.

His tail unwound itself from around me and I swayed. *Why did he put this boulder of a suit on me?* I groaned.

"What do we do now?" I asked him.

"We climb the mountain."

Just a moment or so later my eyes caught something from below. Nervously they darted to Vaughn-ness, his ridge spiked back rippling as his powerful limbs pulled themselves up the mountain. I didn't move and trained my eyes again on what was below. A spark of red fire the color of blood flared up on the peak of a sand dune.

That patch of flame has to be at least the size of my fist, I wondered.

The spark died out. Before the blink of an eye, it reappeared as a swirling blaze of flame that was rapidly stretching in width and height. My knees buckled as the flaming vortex plucked boulders of hardened sand out the ground. The sand in turn coalesced into rock as the tornado swelled, twirling faster and faster. The more sand it wrenched out of the earth, the more it added to its rocky exterior. The twister's tail was burning a shade of orange that was brighter than the rest of its body.

"Vaughn-ness! Look!" I screamed as a crevice split the ground under the twister.

"Not now, Zammus."

An enormous blanket of sand was sucked into the thickening tail of the whirlwind. A boulder that had to have been the size of a horse was flung out of the armored, flaming shell of the storm. A thick crackling tongue of flame struck out of the vortex. The fiery whip lashed the sand and it glazed.

"Vaughn-ness! Turn around! Now!" I yelled in terror.

"Zammus, we have to climb this mountain."

My heart froze as the storm closed the few hundred yards that separated it from the mountain.

"It's pretty hot up here! How did that happen so quickly?" Vaughn-ness chuckled, still looking forward at the mountain.

My once cool skin was now immersed in a thick coat of sticky, slippery sweat. The sound of rock slashing on rock filled the air as the revolving stones of the tornado ground one another to pieces. This thunderous cacophony of rock on rock and the relentless waves of unbelievable heat brought my spirit to its knees. *We're going to be massacred here and he doesn't even know it!* I cursed.

"VAUGHN-NESS! BEHIND YOU!" I screeched.

"What?" he turned his head. "Oh my . . ." His eyes were glass and at their center was the crackling orange heart of the vortex. "Not even . . . I can stop that."

The hundreds of rocks that wrapped around the tornado in concentric rings howled as they ground against each other. The whirlwind swelled like a tidal wave and with a shrill ear-bleeding whine that brought pain to every bone in my body, it flared red and I was blinded by a piercing white light. A boulder erupted from within the storm like a cannon-ball. Following it was a tentacle of orange flame that wound around the stone missile. And both were going to strike Vaughn-ness straight in the face.

"VAUGHN-NESS! NOOOOO!"

Lava burst within my chest and a storm within my soul raged. Despite the impossible, cumbersome weight of the stone armor, I leaped straight up in the air, arms outstretched, and was engulfed by a wave of unfathomable heat and relentless fire. I was inevitably crushed, the stone armor shattering and cracking all around me. *Oooouuughhhh urwwwww* . . . my broken mind moaned from within as my blood pooled under me. Eager and effulgent flames were dancing upon the broken, fragmented armor. *I can't feel anything,* my thoughts oozed. Burying my smashed body, swallowing my widespread arms, and pinning my palms underneath it was the burning boulder.

"Zammus!" I half heard Vaughn-ness yell.

Break it! Just like it tried to break you! a voice ordered in my head. *Destroy it!* the voice commanded. My mind burst like a tomato and was scattered into a million places. A primitive guttural howl started within the base of my lungs. I writhed in anguish as my limbs wickedly contorted. I felt the boulder immobilizing me shake and crack. Having successfully broken the rock, the first parts of my body slid out.

"Zammus? Oh my!" Vaughn-ness gasped as my arm reached out. It was completely covered in gray rocky stone scales and ended in claws.

Oceans of gray rock rushed over me, drowning out my human flesh, while the cracked remnants of armor that still clung to me disintegrated. My teeth violently bit each other, molars slashing on enamel, as vines of stone spiraled through the canals of my veins and over the mountains of my cells. A rocky musculature hewed and chiseled from granite emerged from the marrow of my bones. Shards of obsidian shot up like hairs from my new skin. Hardened clay swirled over my form in rich oranges, reds, and whites. From within myself an avalanche of metamorphosis dissipated my core; my innards lurched and erupted like gunfire.

I flung the boulder's remains off of me. Climbing out, I stood tall. I flexed my hand, retracting granite claws. My gray, rocky granite skin shimmered dully, strangely under the suns.

"How can this be? How can I be? This?" I pondered aloud, flexing and marveling at my new stone digits.

"Zammus? Are you alright?" Vaughn-ness croaked.

"Yes, quite."

"What happened? I saw a blue light pour from under the boulder where you lay. It swarmed over the rock and broke it in two and this thing, your arm, not as it quite is now, slid out. And now you are changed," Vaughn-ness shivered.

"I don't know. How could I?" I answered honestly,

absently watching the fire rock tornado, now a mile away, as it blazed over the neighboring mountains.

Clarity flooded into my mind, like golden water in a desert.

"Vaughn-ness, I have to rescue my humble, benevolent master and his sapphire daughter, An-u. And I need you to help me," I declared.

His purple, lapis lazuli eyes regarded me gently like oceans, "Very well. But what of the mountain and its secrets?"

"I have the feeling that we are going to be coming here again. And if we don't, then I'll have to live without them and figure them out on my own. Now we must go," I spoke.

"Where?"

"East of these mountains."

How do I know that? I questioned myself. *I don't know. Good question,* I quickly thought back.

Above something caught my gaze. My eyes glared into the sky, squinting, focusing. "Wait, do you see that faint shimmering speck in the sky that's shooting over that river?"

"Yes, I see it. But, how can you? Goodness me! What is that?" Vaughn-ness shook, rattling his scales.

My eyes watched the blue shimmer fall to the valleys of the trees below, launching sand hundreds of feet into the air all around it. A faint glimmering hope that could be completely and entirely wrong flickered in my chest. An ember of existence. An-u.

"We're going to see what landed there and why. Ready?" I spoke.

Vaughn-ness's eye ridges narrowed, "Indeed."

I let loose the transformation that I was holding back as I surged forward. Claws of gray and white obsidian leapt from my fingers. Mountains of rock and stone muscle puffed out of me, squeezing and compressing my sides. My arms shot forward, reaching for the ground and eagerly slapping it as I adjusted my running gait. My back stretched, expanding like a spring as it transformed into an armored dome. Powerful back legs shot out behind me like bricks, a tail burst into being like a fetus and slapped the air. White shards spiked viciously all over my body as I galloped, swelling with purpose down the mountain.

"Couldn't I just fly us there?" Vaughn-ness weighed, his talons tearing the stone alongside me.

I shook my head. "Too risky," I told myself.

"Just what are you, Zammus Dre' Suel?" Vaughn-ness breathed.

I roared, laughing in delight. With relish and ease my stone limbs blazed down the mountainside, quickly calculating sharp turns, twisting maneuvers, halting at death drops and cliff hangs, always reconfiguring a new route. My body always ahead of my brain. My stone paws eagerly embraced the sand at the base of the mountain. I allowed myself a deep breath and continued surging forward. I looked to Vaughn-ness, barely behind me, his gargantuan limbs always keeping stride, our dancing paws making the ground blow up in clouds of sand.

The river where the speck had sailed over was just a dot in my vision. With renewed vigor I pushed my limbs forward. I turned my head back, grunting at Vaughn-ness.

"Where are we going?" he questioned, still moving.

I half grunted and growled in reply.

To An-u, I hope. But I don't know. And if you're wrong?

My consciousness refused to answer. Through the desert we raced on, darting around the krystal towers that pockmarked its surface. With relentless eyes I scanned the brightness of their spires, ever watching for signs of life, possible confrontations, and potential threats. The suns above us had painted the spanning dunes a deep ocher by the time we reached the river, an orange snake that wound itself clandestinely over, beneath, and round the dunes. I stopped and padded by its bank.

My head dipped into the liquid magma, greedily swallowing the fire, cherishing its energy, its life. I heard Vaughn-ness savoring its lusciousness beside me.

"I know this river," he said suddenly, ripping his head from its edge. "This is the Imperengú. In the Basilisk tongue it means 'the dancing molten river,'" he gasped in awe.

I lifted my head to regard him, squinting strangely at how my vision narrowed down my snout. My head drifted back to the river, eager for more. Pensive sky-blue eyes peered into me, a tongue of the same light color lolled out of my mouth.

Who am I? What am I? I briefly thought.

In a moment we were back to sprinting; we blazed alongside the spine of the river. We rushed on, just as ceaseless as before. The ominous towers of krystal dwindling, the sand beneath our feet gave way to pebbles that hugged the river's edge as we burned it with our feet. As the suns spread their violet cloak over the land, an emerald forest came into view at the edge of the horizon.

We're almost there, just a little further. An-u, I really hope you're there, I thought, ragged.

I grunted to Vaughn-ness that we increase our speed.

"How is that even possible?" he asked, but quickened his gait.

Throughout the darkening of the night, as the weavers of the stars changed the canvas of the night to blue, indigo, purple and black, we ran on. By the pinks that were painted across the skies signaling the dawn, we made our way into the forest. Trees made of glowing emerald shrouded us in salutations. The krystal ground was quivering everywhere and sending up bellowing tongues of white clear smoke.

That's why, I thought.

Ahead, over the edge of a monstrous crater, lay the body of An-u. I ran over to her, my body changing and shrinking. I was back on two legs and made of flesh.

"You know her?" Vaughn-ness asked.

"Yes," I said, wrapping my arms around her, cradling her body. "An-u, look at me. Please wake up. It's Zammus."

Her body felt cool against my arms.

"This was in the crater, alongside the debris," Vaughn-ness said, coming forward with a cloak draping over his snout.

"Thank you, Vaughn-ness! Her skin is freezing! But that could be because she's not warm blooded like me."

"Perhaps," he concurred.

An-u shivered as I wrapped the cloak over her.

How did you get here? What brought you here? I thought.

"Who is this? Why is she here? What's going on? How did you change back there? Why are we here? Answer me, Zammus!" Vaughn-ness erupted.

I paused, tightening my grip on An-u's limbs. My lower back was stiff and felt incredibly dense, as did my shoulders. I looked at my fingers creeping over An-u's calves and froze, taking a deep breath. The tips were grayish white and made of stone permanently, like my shoulder.

"I'd like some answers, Zammus," Vaughn-ness growled. His features quickly morphing and becoming feral as his scales rose up, protruding out from all over his body like thorns. His claws flashed as he thrust his face into mine.

"Tell me everything. From the beginning. About what's going on here! Now!" He demanded. "And if you don't, it's simple. I'm leaving," he sat back on his haunches, staring down at me imperially. His emerald eye ridges, usually circular were narrowed down to triangles.

"I–I–I . . ."

"You're on a quest!" he boomed. "That's as obvious as the suns. We're going to be in this forest for quite the while. You might as well make yourself comfortable," he breathed.

Sighing with anticipation, I put An-u down gently and sat beside her, looking up into Vaughn-ness's face.

"I should have told you this from the beginning when we met. I am from a place called London; it's where I was born. It's a city in the country of Britain which exists on a continent called Europe. I know that means nothing to you."

"Actually, it is quite fascinating! I know of countries and continents; Terra Draco has its own. But do go on," Vaughn-ness remarked.

"All of these places are on a world called Earth. On an island I found a piece of metal, a jewel actually, in a treasure hoard underground. Once I touched it, it grew a life of its own, forcefully wrapped itself around me, and transported me here to your world. Not a second after my arrival, a big fat yellow dragon wanted to kill me, though I didn't know it was a dragon then. Other dragons watched as if the two of us were competing in a tournament. I don't know how, but I managed to hold my own and kill it. By then, the spectating dragons were gone. I don't know why they didn't rip me to shreds; I was in horrible shape and soaked in purple blood.

"I lost consciousness and when I came to, I was in an arena packed with dragons. I had to fight three or four of the beasts. Mind you, that the thing that brought me here was still with me, on my chest. During my second skirmish, in the arena, it was accidentally activated. I was transformed into a dragon, though not permanently. I fled and wandered the lands, meeting two of the three companions you met earlier. The metal on my chest destroyed itself, killing me. I met the dragon Jaow-kieen the moment I entered this spirit realm. He told me I'm here to kill and destroy Maldroto. He was training me. The woman beside me is his daughter as well as the sorcerous means that brought me here. The three of us were separated.

"The next thing I knew, I was in prison. I escaped. You know the rest," I finished.

Vaughn-ness's jaws opened and closed twice.

"Jaow-kieen is here! How can that be? I've searched this realm for over fifty millennia. As well as the other one, where the spirits come from, the physical plane. No one has seen him since the end of the war when Maldroto was imprisoned. Speaking of that–"

"You knew Jaow-kieen?! How did you know him?" I asked, excited.

"Of course I knew him, my boy. I trained him to fight in the wars. I was great friends with his parents and once they were . . . killed, I took him under my care. I taught him all the branches of the vast tree that comprises science and technology. I paid his one-thousand-year degree for elite flame practitioning and thermodynamic chemical engineering. For the first six thousand years of his life, I mentored him. We fought alongside each other in the millions of years that this planet was at war. And then he vanished. This is the first I hear of him since. He's like a grandson to me."

"Not a son?" I asked carefully.

"No. When I was made the first dragon by the scaled goddess Ostraya, I was a great tortoise of five hundred or so years of age before she gave me a new form. From the touch of her omnipotence, I was first transformed into the being you see now. From that day on, wherever I left a trail of my four footprints, a dragon would form from the track of my paws. That's not really how it happened, but that's beside the point. These were my first daughters and sons. And so, the first few hundreds of us lived for trillions of years before Maldroto ravaged the planet, when there was both water and fire on this world. When there were plants of flesh, not just krystal. When there were creatures with water, ice, earth, and even plants in their blood.

"Not just fire. Maldroto destroyed them all. This world was not always just fire as you see it now. Nor was flame the only type of life," Vaughn-ness lamented, pink tears dripping from his eyes and gliding down his snout.

"I have to kill him! Destroy him!" I said raising my voice.

Deep, deep rumbling shook the air and vibrated through the ground, shaking the green krystal trees around us as Vaughn-ness wholeheartedly laughed.

"You?! You! How? If all of Terra Draco's armies, the six races, the Anuras, myself as well as the entire planet could not even come close to killing or weakening him, merely subduing after millions of years of fighting, what makes you–you tiny, infinitesimal, minuscule thing–think that you alone can kill, destroy, and obliterate him and his existence?! PAH! You are a fool, the emperor of fools!" Vaughn-ness spat, laughing boisterously, golden tears flying from his eyes.

"I don't know," I said, curling into a ball. "Can't you help me? You were touched by a god. You have that power in your veins!" I begged.

"I apologize, Zammus, but I'm afraid I'm not strong enough. I'm only a dragon and an elder at that."

"Is it really that pointless? That impossible?" I sighed, dejected, hanging my head in despair.

"Yes, let me show you what you're up against," Vaughn-ness said grimly as his claws raked the ground.

"But he's coming back, though," I said crestfallen.

"What?! Terra Draco will go extinct!" Vaughn-ness roared, his wings spread open in fear, his tail taut as a rope and his breathing coming in rasps. "We won't survive this time! We can't survive that!" He nervously spat a ball of golden flame at his feet.

"It's because of me. The sorcery that brought me here was made on this planet. It has returned. Its presence will weaken Maldroto's bonds and he'll be free," I gasped, my heart racing.

"How did you come by this knowledge? How do I know that which you claim is true?" Vaughn-ness growled, pacing and flicking his tail, clearly not having listened to everything I had said.

I took a deep breath, my brow and palms dripping in sweat as I continuously balled and opened my fists.

"Jaow-kieen told me. Trust him! Ask him all the details. He knows better than I do."

"We need to find him; we have to," he announced.

"I know. Don't worry, we will. You were going to tell me about Maldroto," I said, catching something reflective from the corner of my eye.

I walked over to the shining source and laid my eyes over an ornate, arabesque bow encased in white krystal that mirrored its shape.

"I was the first to see Maldroto arrive on Terra Draco and the very first to engage him."

My fingers wrapped around the bow and I gazed back at Vaughn-ness.

"Come close, let me show you," Vaughn-ness beckoned me with a wave of his paw. Hesitantly I came forward as he touched a scale on his eye ridge to the top of my head. There was a flash of piercing white light. I saw nothing but blackness.

"Millions of years ago," his voice echoed, though I couldn't see him.

The afterimage faded and my vision returned. Green fields were everywhere from horizon to horizon. Flat grassy plains were all around me. An ear splitting, piercing noise tormented the air. Something was falling out the sky, a spinning blue, purple and black mass. The whine of the spiraling mass escalated in pitch and in a revolving eruption of green and purple light the wrenching missile crashed into the earth, shooting a curtain of black thorny blades in all directions as it slid, razing a path of absolute devastation. Oily black tendrils radiated from it, crawling out of the ground like tentacles.

Like spiders they crept out of the deep fissure. The shape burst, dissolving into transparent black vapor. The black mist hovered over the crater and collapsed into black muck. The melted substance pulsed and from it rose an outstretched silver and purple hand. Slender fingers clutched at the earth; instantly it turned the same oily black and oozed. A head of the same silvery-purple complexion, framed by long black-and steel-colored hair emerged; a body followed. Around the impact crater tooth-white flames were sweltering in the grass. Black jagged blades of lightning were hovering around the figure. Black liquid was dripping from its bare flesh. It was very tall with four arms and improbably covered in thick, long muscles. It was male. Blue, silver, and white light shone with omnipotence from its eyes.

"Fair day. A glorious afternoon, is it not?"

A cold silence responded in turn.

"Why do you gawk at me like a fool, dragon?" the figure asked Vaughn-ness, who wasn't that far off.

As an emerald god is how he stood, as gold flecks of luminescence danced over him. His scales were rigid, his limbs thick, his stance as firm as a mountain. And his eyes, blue and purple, were hard and cold as krystal daggers.

"What do you want here?" he growled, his voice echoing across the plains.

"Nothing and everything," the being barked just as loud. A wind swept up and carried his words. "Will you help me attain it?" it asked, softly, not a glimmer nor needle of a threat in its voice.

"No," Vaughn-ness announced without a moment of doubt.

"Already you then seal your fate," the creature announced evenly and coolly.

Kneeling on one knee it thrust a hand into the earth, twisting it deeply. Shockwaves of blackness glided across the expanse of plains in seconds. The green earth was gone, replaced by pitch-black fields. Dead, lifeless, barren, burnt, and scorched all around for as far as the eye could see.

"Who are you? What are you?" Vaughn-ness demanded with a roar.

Standing up the being answered, "I am Maldroto. Now what I am is not an ounce of your concern."

A jagged blade of arcing black lightning shot from his fingers, crackling and slicing the air, racing to meet Vaughn-ness. With a swipe of his arm, Vaughn-ness froze the forking black tendrils of light, encasing their branches in a flat prism of clear white krystal. The krystalized lightning plummeted to the blackened earth and shattered to useless fragments of silver dust.

"You're clever! I like you!" Maldroto bellowed, grinning with gusto and relish.

"Do not flatter with me with polite lies of fair play," Vaughn-ness roared eloquently.

He tilted his wide paw upwards and spat, breathing wild white flames into it. The eager effulgent flames wrapped completely around his paw, crackling as they encased his knuckles, claws, and forearm. From across the blackened field bright purple light infused with flooding molten golden rays were wrapping around two of Maldroto's left fists.

"Let me show you creation, good drake. And may you be humble in your learning," called Maldroto as he shot off the ground, the two fists on his left side blazing as merciless suns as he flared, surging towards Vaughn-ness.

"I will do no learning or studying under you," Vaughn-ness growled as he closed his glowing paw into a fist. His thick powerful back legs propelled him off the ground. The emerald shields of his wings flashed, pouring from his back like cascading waterfalls. The blades of his wings sliced up the ground beneath him with katanas of air as he shot forward to meet him, his flaming white paw glowing as furiously as a star.

"What rapture!" Maldroto grinned.

The two entities collided as two celestial bodies as they clashed in a titanic wave of blinding, scorching light. The eruption of energy from their fists bellowed into a shimmering hot, purple and golden-white orb that was growing bigger than the both of them. It burst like a water droplet and threw the two apart, repelling them in separate directions like opposing stones. Viciously uncontrollable tidal waves of air hurled them upon the dead earth, their forms slicing deep, long furrows into the bruised, raw earth.

Suddenly all was black. I couldn't make out anything in the darkness, then just as abruptly, lights pierced my vision. The thick spike-edged eye ridge of Vaughn-ness was all my eyes could see.

Grunting he pulled back and I fell onto my backside, completely disoriented.

"There was nothing left . . . of that place," Vaughn-ness sighed.

"Where was that?" I asked.

"It became known as the Urn Fire Desert. Do you see now, Zammus? He poisoned the land and it can never return to the way it was to this very day. If anything, it only spread. And the wars simply made it even worse. There's nothing green left here," Vaughn-ness lamented. I bowed my head and kept silent out of respect for his loss.

"That's enough of the past for now. Get some rest, you look like you're going to faint. I'll watch over you and her," he gestured to An-u with his snout. "Do you think she'll wake up?" he asked, eying her with interest. "I've never seen anyone or anything that's made of krystal. How fascinating. What a mystery," he remarked.

"Hopefully she comes to after I do!" I said yawning.

I couldn't comprehend how suddenly tired I felt. I stretched my arms behind my head and stretched out in the pleasantly warm dirt.

"Wake me if need be, please," I yawned.

Vaughn-ness dipped his head. My eyes closed.

Sweet dreams, my mind sung to me.

12

Orchestration; A Subsequent Act; No Intermission

An armadillo lay at my feet, happily wagging its armored tail.

"I remember you, little fellow," I smiled, extending my hand.

It licked at me eagerly.

"You weren't this big last time, though," I remarked. "May I?" I asked, gently resting my hands on the dome of its armored back.

It lapped at my hand in response.

"Okay, I guess that's 'yes,'" I grinned, gently picking up the armadillo and placing it on my thigh where it curled up and nuzzled.

It had grown, though. The first time I had seen it, it was the size of a watermelon. Now it had become the size of a carriage wheel. My fingers ran over its armored back and in doing so, a thought struck me. *Now that's very strange. The texture of its plates feels just as hard as wood.*

"How did you come to see me?" I said, thinking back to our initial encounter. The armadillo flicked an ear. "Where did you come from, Armadillo?"

Small black eyes regarded me. They were soft, obscured, and thoughtful. My little friend squealed and bounded off of me, galloping ahead like a miniature horse.

"Wait up, Armadillo! Where are you going?" I said, starting after it.

Looking around for the first time I saw that stone ruins surrounded us and farther up ahead lay a single black hillock. After several dozen paces we were mounting the crest. My friend rolled onto his back, his tongue lolling out. As I came to stand on the peak, I looked all around me and peered into the valley below.

"Why did you bring me here?" I whispered.

Red krystal trees littered the landscape. A shadow shot up from below, throwing me off my feet.

"Zammus Dre' Suel! You will die!" bellowed the darkness as it spread itself impossibly wider, its immaterial sides stretching ever outward like a manta ray. Sharp piercing squeals of horror shook my ears as the armadillo keened.

I quickly had him in my arms, my fingers stroking his arrow-shaped head.

"Who are you? Who sent you? And what do you want?" I demanded, even though I was shaking like a trembling leaf.

The shadow pulsed and throbbed, swelling as onyx muscles possessed it. Shapes congealed and pooled and before long I was staring at a jet-black ebony dragon, floating in midair, the curtains of its wings fully extended.

"I am here to kill you and all those you care about," it spoke with marrow-chilling cold. "Starting with that pathetic crying pillow of yours."

"No!" I yelled.

"Too late! Haha! Haha! Haha!" bellowed the dragon as a spiral of silver flame spun out of its jaws. I turned my back, shielding my wailing friend with my body.

"NOOOOOO!"

***

"No! No! No!" I cried, violently tossing and turning.

Cold liquid flooded onto my face. "H-H-H-H-HHEHF!" I gasped, shivering as my eyes shot open.

There before me stood An-u in the rain as it painted her with black drops.

"What were you screaming about?" she puzzled, her brow crinkling into a frown.

"Nothing," I dismissed.

"Right," she chewed her lip. "About time you got up," she said, looking down at me with hard eyes until slowly her krystalline features split into a smile and then a grin. She extended a hand.

"You're one to talk," I grinned back, taking her hand.

"How did you two find me?"

"We saw you fall. The dragon here, Vaughn-ness and I saw something blue racing through the sky. And then it plummeted. There was a sliver of hope that it could have been you. So we followed it," I said.

An-u nodded, her bright eyes squinting as she bit her lips, thinking. "I was imprisoned, Zammus. At the bottom of this giant rectangular pit—"

"You were too?!"

"Tell me first!" An-u pleaded.

I considered this. “We both woke up in prisons after we were attacked and separated.”

“Who put us there and why? We have to find my father!” An-u announced.

“We have company!” barked Vaughn-ness.

An-u and I whipped our eyes to the sky. Three very large dragons were spiraling down. An-u grabbed her bow and I retrieved my staff.

“Do you know who they are? Not friends, I presume,” Vaughn-ness ventured.

“We’ve been acquainted,” An-u snarled.

“Unfortunately,” I added.

The giants landed, one white, a brown, and a silver.

“Oh, look, Grath, the two runts found each other!” gloated the white beast that had thrown me off of Jaow-kieen’s back so long ago.

“It’s useless and pointless, Croinen, they’ll ain’t never find the big ‘un,” the silver one snarled.

“Ain’t that roight, Yagsaer?” growled the brown brute, glaring at me with sick orange yellow eyes.

“Exactectly,” the silver dragon beamed.

Vaughn-ness’s scales stood out from his body like blades. “All of you will leave here if you’re wise,” he hissed, golden energy oozing from his scales to dance over his body as he bared his fangs.

“You stole him! Where is he?” An-u howled.

“Where is Jaow-kieen? Who sent you? And what do you want?” I growled through gritted teeth, as the staff changed into a sledgehammer.

“That’s a nice trick, Nawga! I want me one!” hissed the white dragon, leaping at me. “Capture them all!” it spat.

I leapt through the air, lunging forward, raising my hammer. My ears caught the twang of An-u's bowstring and the swoosh of her arrow. The white dragon's blue eyes swelled like water as it released an eager shrill.

I'm going to kill you for what you've done, I thought.

Suddenly the hammer flew out of my hand and dissolved, disappearing into blue smoke and sparks.

"What the?!–How?!" I gasped.

Completely unbalanced without the hammer, I clumsily sunk through the air only to be jammed by the edge of the dragon's wing. The air left my body. Swinging the wall of its paw, it batted me.

"Staff, why have you deserted me?" I panicked.

Above me Vaughn-ness and the brown dragon were swooping in a knot of complex aerial maneuvers, locked in combat.

"You're pathetically piteous!" my attacker scowled, slapping me out of the air with its tail and into the ground. "To think that you could exist and even hold your own against a dragon!" howled my assailant.

I lay on my back, dazed for a moment.

In that split second, I saw the means that An-u's bow served as I watched her pull the bowstring and an arrow of light pulsed into life, manifesting from nothing. As it blazed it erupted with power, racing and shooting forward on a golden tether that yanked her body along through the air in its path. I leapt to my feet and took off running towards the emerald krystal grasses.

"Where are you going? That's no fun!" roared the beast as it swung its tail right behind me. I spun, stiffening my body for the blow and embraced it. My arms and legs wrapped around the thick muscular cord.

"Get off of me, vermin!" the dragon roared, snapping its tail forward.

I lost my grip and flew forward, landing on the thin membrane along the edge of its opened wing.

"Stone fingers, let's see if you're good at anything!" I said, digging my hands into the soft gray membrane and ripping it like parchment.

"AHHH! Damn you! Bastard! OOOOUUEE!" wailed the beast, spinning and flying out of control.

Purple fluid was spraying onto my arms and face. I threw the rest of my body on the wing and continued to slice and shear it apart with my fingers. Wailing in agony, the dragon wildly careened and collapsed onto its side, completely crushing its undamaged wing with a sickening *CRUNCH!* and *SPLUNK!* The devastating impact threw me dozens of meters away from my enemy.

"Mission accomplished! You're now flightless," I groaned, roughly tumbling and bouncing across the ground.

Purple blood was flowing all over its back and shoulders.

"You will die for this, Inferior! I will kill you and rip your bones from your body and then every muscle and tendon from your remains!" bellowed the wretch.

I leapt to my feet as it lunged at me and blue flames left its jaws in a trail of spiraling death. I dove to the ground in avoidance and viciously rolled on my side like a log. My fingers made contact with something long and very thick. I stopped rolling and inspected it.

"A rope!" I exclaimed.

The angry pounding of my killer echoed not far behind. Starting to my feet, I quickly examined the rope. It was a dark green, as thick as my whole body, yet surprisingly light. The rest of the rope extended for meters upon meters in thick loops and vanished into the ground. My antagonist swiped at me with his forepaw. But I was quick, and I was ready. As it jumped through the air I leapt, throwing the rope over its claws. The rope latched onto the thick wrist and with a yank of its swinging arm, the dragon tugged the rope and threw me onto its arm. Wasting not a moment I darted over the road of its forearm, throwing the rope over, under and between the round boulder-sized outer muscles.

TWACK! Its tail struck me with the force of an earthquake. I was deposited on its back. Thank goodness the rope was still in my hands! I darted over and across its back, adrenaline enabling me to gracefully dodge and leap over spines. Out of breath I arrived at its neck. I dove over the side and, forcing a deep bellowing breath, I swung under the neck, tucking my legs. I contracted every part of my body and thrust my legs straight out to swing myself up and land on the dragon's nape.

"What are you doing to me, most foul demon?!" the beast howled, shaking its head from side to side while wriggling its neck. In that manner, it dragged me and the rope up and over, wrapping the fiber several times around its neck as I swung around to-and-fro. Dizzy and disoriented, I lost my grip and fell to the ground.

Get up! Now's your only chance! My thoughts urged me on. Shakily and feeling broken I rose. Beside me was a clump of knotted rope the size of a carriage.

"Where are you, fiend?!" bellowed the dragon, shaking with rage and pain some distance behind me, but looking in the opposite direction.

A pillar of stone and krystal stood right in front of me. It was covered in spikes, ridges, and arcing circles and loops. The ground beneath it was a clear, translucent white and the krystalline growths appeared to extend a great distance into the earth.

"Let's go! Now or never!" I said to myself.

Grunting with effort, I hurled the coiling knot of rope over the structure. *I hope this krystal holds! I hope this works!* I stressed, puffing my cheeks.

I turned around and saw the dragon turn at the same time. Its blue eyes stabbed into me like spears.

"Hey, you big stupid reptile! Come and kill me! If you dare!" I taunted.

Onwards it scrabbled, its legs charging the earth, the sound of its tether smoothly swooshing through the air. My feet kicked dirt off the ground as I ran. The land ahead of me was running out. A quick cliff face was just a few breaths before me.

"INFIDEL!!!!" screeched the beast.

My legs left the edge of the cliff.

"VERMIN!" the dragon howled, leaping off the cliff.

My legs jackknifed through the air.

"INFERIOR!!! MAY DEATH SLICE YOU INTO A THOUSAND–URGHH! HFEHFFGLURSPH!!!"

The sound of cracking stone and a chopped tree plummeting to the ground filled the air as the noose tightened around the dragon. It violently shuddered, tensing every muscle. Then it was still. My legs fell into a small depression in the cliff wall. And there I stood, catching my breath and staring at the body as it leaned against the cliff wall, a hung dragon. Purple blood oozed lazily from between its jaws. *The others!* I thought, concerned. Quickly I climbed up the crags of the cliff face and pulled myself over the edge.

"I'm impressed," An-u observed. "Having the dragon hang itself, unawares. Your setup was quite clever."

I looked at her. She had barely a scratch on her. Her hands and feet were soaked with the purple of her enemy. Her deep azure blue hair cascaded in wild waves to her hips. The wind rustled her tattered black knee-length cloak. The bow clutched tightly in her hand was lightly dripping violet blood.

"Have you seen Vaughn-ness?" I asked.

A long blue shimmer materialized in my hand.

"Of all times and now you choose to return to me!" I stormed angrily.

The staff sympathetically shrunk into a sorrowful clasp that clamped over my wrist.

"It disappeared before the battle even started!" I explained.

Deep bellowing shook the air as Vaughn-ness came into view. He was carrying the brown dragon in his jaws.

"Let me go! How dare an elder humiliate a peak dragon like me! I'm young and strong, I'm supposed to surpass you in all accounts! This is blasphemous! You're a product of the darkest, vilest, utmost blasphemy!" whined the dragon.

Vaughn-ness landed on the ground and dropped the fiend from his jaws. Howling in indignant humiliation, the beast clattered to the ground, landing in a piteous heap. Before it could gather its senses, Vaughn-ness placed a paw over its body, pinning it to the ground. The brown brute struggled, breathing heavily.

"Release me! Release me! Release me, I say!"

Vaughn-ness bellowed, "You are going to tell us who sent you and everything you know."

"Starting with why you and your friends tried to kill us," I spoke.

"My name is Grath. Aseroph sent us. We all serve Lord V'rossar. Out of fear, though. We don't know what he is or where he comes from. None of us do. But he controls us. And destroys any dragon that opposes him," the brown dragon gulped, speaking slowly.

An-u, Vaughn-ness, and I exchanged confused and nervous glances. Silence hung over the four of us for a moment.

"Why did you attack Jaow-kieen and the two of us earlier?" I spoke, gesturing to An-u and myself.

"Where is he?" An-u asked.

Grath huffed, breathing a streaming column of air from his nostrils. His eyes closed as he spoke.

"Lord V'rossar believes that he will come back. The Eradicator. We worship him. Our Lord believes that he will return reborn."

Grath's words silenced my heart. *Maldroto,* I thought.

"When the Eradicator returns, he will pass through five phases. The Judge, the Executioner, the Destroyer, the Liberator, and the Creator. He will finish what he started millions of years past before he was conquered. Before his fall."

I looked to meet Vaughn-ness's eye. He was shaking his head from side to side, raking his free paw in the dirt.

"You, creature!" Grath coughed at me. "Are the reason we attacked you. The reason the red and gold warrior dragon is imprisoned and being tortured. The Lord V'rossar has been watching you, searching for you. You are a prized jewel to him."

I gulped, swallowing uncertainly. A lump was forming in my throat.

"You are giving the Eradicator strength. Strength to rise. And he wants to know why, how," Grath paused to breathe.

"Once he gets a hold of you, he intends to find a way to see if he can use you as a means to accelerate the return of the Eradicator. Most eternally and infinitely revered Maldroto," he finished.

Silence drowned us all. An-u was the first to react.

"Although there is no way to measure how much you say is truth or lie, you are going to take my friends and I to meet this V'rossar."

She quickly loosed an arrow into Grath's flank.

Whoah! Wow! I shouted to myself, eyeing Grath's pierced thigh. Her arrow had completely buried itself in his leg. All that could be seen was a golden translucent cord, tethering him to An-u's ghastly bow. *Where did she get such a savage thing like that?* I questioned. Vaughn-ness's saucer wide eyes mirrored my shock.

"Damn it, you nasty wench! How was that even really necessary?!" Grath howled, grimacing, as his tail and leg broke into writhing spasms.

"Yeah, An-u, you didn't have to do that. He's been answering all our questions and hasn't at all been aggressive about it," I protested.

I really didn't like that she had done that. Although he was on the enemy's side, he still deserved to be treated humanely. Her causing him pain was unjustified. Had he been attacking us and life threatening, I could understand. But here he was completely calm, complacent, feeding us information, not to mention pinned under the boulder of Vaughn-ness's paw.

"I agree with Zammus, An-u. Grath has not been confrontational. Your lack of ethical treatment is not a fair or equal exchange, given his polite and composed mannerisms in assisting us by providing enlightening answers to our questions. My dear," Vaughn-ness looked An-u in the eye, "Use force and draw blood only if you need to and as a last resort. Just because you can doesn't mean you have to. And just because you could doesn't mean you should. Your torturing of him is wrong."

An-u stared at Vaughn-ness and I, glowering at us with cold icy eyes and an expressionless face.

"Hmph," she grunted, keeping the blades of her eyes stabbing into me.

"There are other ways to get him to do things. Nicer ways," I said, not backing down from An-u's death glare.

For a while not an ounce of her wavered.

"Fine," she said softly, angrily.

Vaughn-ness hummed. I walked over to Grath and climbed onto his leg. My fingers wrapped around the thin rope protruding from him.

"Hey, Grath, this is going to hurt some. Probably a lot. Just don't knock me out with that tail of yours," I said, raising my voice, and warily eyeing the leg-length and scimitar-shaped spines dotting every surface of it.

"You smell like dragon," was all he said.

"Brace yourself," I warned.

Taking a deep breath I tugged. A shrill piercing growl rattled my ears. His baneful tail began thrashing back and forth.

"Vaughn-ness! Get him under control!" I yelled.

"Oulaura Vöcis!" An-u said, flicking her palm.

The tail fell to the ground and stayed limp. Completely shocked and confused, my eyes met hers for a moment. Her gaze had softened a little bit. I pulled harder and fell back, landing by his tail, as blood jetted out and soaked me. An arrow the length of my body was dangling on the rope in my hand. Grath roared loudly in what had to be pain, relief, or both.

"Thank you! Thank you!" he sighed.

The arrow bucked, flying sideways and dragging me along.

"Hey! What the–" I yelled as I was hauled through the dirt.

The rope disappeared from my hands. There was a clicking and snapping noise and I found myself face to face with An-u's sapphire toes. From above An-u smirked and, chuckling softly, she backed away.

"Are you well, Zammus?" Vaughn-ness asked through his vibrating laugh.

"Yeah! I'm good!" I groaned, dazed.

Shakily I pushed myself onto my hands, gathered myself, and stood up. An-u's eyes were azure halfmoons as she smirked at me, her shoulders jumping as she lightly laughed. Even though I was covered in blood, I managed to give her a half smile.

"Grath," I spoke walking over to meet his face.

"Creature," his orange yellow eyes beckoned to me.

"V'rossar wants me. Follow your orders. Take me to him," I said.

"But . . .?" Grath questioned, at odds with conflicted feelings. "You are the liberator of the arrow."

"Zammus?" Vaughn-ness questioned.

An-u said nothing, her eyes downcast, thinking.

I stared Vaughn-ness in the eye, "We're going to rescue her father, my mentor, and your grandson."

Behind me An-u gasped.

I gave her a brief glance that said we would all talk about this later.

"Plus," I continued, "We all have a score to settle with this V'rossar. I'm as eager to meet him as he is me."

"Please take us, Grath. You know full well that dragons can vibrate their bodies fast enough to transport themselves across vast distances. Do not deny it," I said.

"Oh. Fine," he growled, defeated. "Hold on tight," he said with reluctance.

An-u came up beside me and snaked her arms around one of Grath's claws. Beside her I followed suit. Vaughn-ness coiled his tail around us. He looped the rest of it over Grath's arm. Vaughn-ness looked at me, and I nodded.

"We're ready," he spoke.

I gently leaned my shoulder into An-u's.

"Here we go! Hold tight!" yelled Grath.

Every brown scale on his body tremored and danced until he was a blur. The rapid oscillation was hammering my jaw. I felt An-u thrumming beside me, her shoulder grinding against mine. My stomach felt sick. An erupting pulse swarmed through Grath's body. The ground beneath us vanished. A heartbeat later, I was thrown into a black obsidian tiled floor, utterly dazed. Ferocious roaring pierced the air, exploding.

"FATHER!" An-u screamed running.

I leapt to my feet and started after her. Vaughn-ness shook himself like a dog.

"You have a plan?" he asked, raising an eye ridge.

"Nope!" I yelled sprinting past him.

I heard him mutter something and the black walls of the corridor bled green. Vaughn-ness's mammoth paws struck the floor behind me.

"Although he brought us here, I had to make sure Grath couldn't alert the rest of the fortress. Nearly extinct dragon sorcery has him contained in a bubble that traps sound inside and out," he smirked.

We caught up to An-u. *Who'd have thought that krystals could run so fast?* Another roar of pain, louder than the first shook the walls.

"I'll never tell you!" A thunderous voice bellowed.

"Jaow-kieen!" Vaughn-ness and I yelled together.

"He's above us!" Vaughn-ness shouted.

Dark massive shapes materialized before us. Six long sinewy dragons.

"Not to worry!" Vaughn-ness barked, and within the same instant the guards were each floating helplessly in a green bubble of light. We rounded a bend, pausing at an ebony staircase that looked like it was made for a god. The width of the impressive structure mirrored that of a ballroom.

"Hop on," Vaughn-ness instructed, planting us onto his back with a sweeping tail. He bounded up the stairs, leaping up twenty to thirty steps at a time. We encountered no resistance.

How massive is this place and who built it? I wondered, eying the grand elaborate Gothic architecture that showed no signs of ending. A blue light was looming up ahead. I felt An-u tense up beside me. I felt better knowing I wasn't the only one panicking on the inside. Vaughn-ness launched himself off the final steps and propelled us into a chamber that had to be the size of a mosque or a grand temple.

"There's nothing here!" I gasped incredulously.

"Not true. Not true," Vaughn-ness objected.

"Father?" An-u cried out.

Her voice echoed throughout the vast room, shooting off the gray walls and spinning up the domed ceiling, spiraling across its golden surface. The air spat back with mocking silence. A gloating quiet. The stone on my fingers shivered. I slowly climbed down Vaughn-ness's back. I twisted the sapphire clasp off my wrist.

"Show yourself!" Vaughn-ness roared.

The air ignored him.

"V'rossar. Show yourself," I said calmly.

"Thank you for speaking so softly and politely," a voice swirled from behind me, blowing warm breath onto my ear.

I jumped as a shadow appeared seemingly from my back. A very tall black shape walked very closely in front of me. It stopped a respectable yard away, facing me.

"Zammus Dre' Suel. It's a pleasure. I am most honored," V'rossar grinned, proffering a low elegant bow.

Purple eyes glowing, beaming as he extended his arm, inviting me to shake his hand. I stared, motionless, unmistakably refusing. His eyes displayed hurt and his expression grew pained.

"Now, now, there is no need to be so cold and rude, how extremely impolite," he sniffed, aloof.

I stared, my eyes moving over his grotesque and demonic features. He was at least two meters taller than me, with a skull that housed two devilish curling spiraling horns which fragmented into antlers. Hundreds of spines adorned his face and that muscularly bloated neck and torso of his;

wicked spikes, longer than my forearms, savagely protruded from the sides of his arms, starting from the wrist and ending just below the shoulder. His thighs and hind legs were long and heavily muscled like the rest of him. The claws of his hands and feet possessed six digits each and were lengthy like a lizard's. His improbably wide shoulders had an uncontrollable sagging and hunched-over quality to them.

It's as if he were carrying some sort of heavy bundle on his back. Maybe wings?

Behind him, arching through the air was a thick black coil, as ebony as the rest of him. The tail flexed, swimming through the air like a tentacle darting through water. Gruesome knife-length barbs decked its tip like a crown. A baneful spike, the length of a saber, dwarfed all the rest. My eyes returned to his purple gaze. Strong feelings of animosity began to boil in my veins. The figure before me had orchestrated all of my recent hardships: the capture and torture of Jaow-kieen; what I recently understood as the separation of An-u, Jaow-kieen and myself; An-u's imprisonment; my own horribly and unforgettably traumatic convict experience; and the three dragon assassins.

The sapphire in my hand lengthened into a short single-bladed axe.

"Oh, now that's outlandish, quite quaint! Where can I get one?" V'rossar chimed.

"You've clearly been quite the architect of my and all our fates of late," I proclaimed, swinging my arms wide and gesturing to An-u and Vaughn-ness. I slightly motioned to them to remain silent and still.

"I have to admit, you've done an impressive job. Quite excellent," I commended him, smiling.

"Oh, thank you! How sweet of you!" he beamed, flattered, sniffling and pretending to wipe a tear from his eye. He even put a hand on his chest and bowed modestly.

"May our games begin?" I grinned.

"Yes of course, dear friend. After you," he smiled slyly.

"Where is Jaow-kieen?" I smiled.

"Right here of course!" V'rossar leapt, whirling into a theatrical pose, as if he were pulling open a curtain.

When he landed our surroundings were altered, a change in scene. The chamber was the same, but dust, filth and grime covered all its walls, the floor and surfaces. With the illusion gone I was able to see the true architecture of the room. Impressive black and gray Doric columns rose like trees from the floor; many were broken and masonry littered the floor like bird droppings. There were various levels and bridges all over the place. An enormous dark blue sphere the size of half a field was holding Jaow-kieen. One of his legs was dangling, broken. Hundreds–no, thousands–of dragons were prowling on the levels, sneering, saliva dripping from their jaws.

V'rossar turned, spreading his arms like a warm host. "Welcome to Onoguol. My fortress, my citadel. I hope you like it," he smiled warmly.

"Jaow-kieen! We're here!" Vaughn-ness roared.

"We're going to get you out of here!" I yelled.

Within the bubble Jaow-kieen shook frantically. I couldn't tell if it was in pain or fright.

"Father!" An-u yelled, leaving Vaughn-ness's side and sprinting towards her father.

"NO! Why are you here?! Why did you come! He'll kill you! He'll kill all of us!" Jaow-kieen roared, terrorized.

"We'll get out of here alive! We'll survive this! We all will, Father! For you!" An-u howled. "I won't let you die! NEVER!"

She continued surging forward, unshaken with Vaughn-ness backing her, galloping behind her.

"Oh, how very touching," V'rossar sighed, gingerly clutching his chest. "I'll hate for it to be a pity when I have to kill her," he smiled.

He leapt into a low, wide-legged squatting stance.

"Let's dance! Pivot?" he asked, lunging at me.

"Ballroom!" I cried, leaping and swiping with my axe.

"FINISH THEM!" V'rossar roared, niceties and pleasantries discarded.

A whirlwinding avalanching cacophony of flapping wings pierced the air, almost deafening me as thousands of small, human-sized dragons swarmed over An-u and Vaughn-ness.

"An-u! Vaughn-ness!" I yelled as they were overwhelmed, the weight of hundreds pinning them down. Hundreds more kept coming.

V'rossar's fist slammed into my jaw. The blow viciously knocked me to the ground.

"You want me. You have us. Now what? You use me to raise Maldroto? Your stupid cult will fall apart!" I spat, glaring as he stood above me.

I don't know where I got the defiance, but I knew a dumb move like that would cost me. His clawed foot scooped me off the ground and I was launched like a ball. *Yeah, definitely cost me!*

"I hope you all may get to delightfully enjoy your stay," V'rossar hissed.

He leapt a good thirty feet into the air. There was a *whoosh!* as four huge wings struck out from his back.

Great. This sucks, I cursed. He sped over to my airborne body. He grabbed me by the ankle and threw me down. The ground was coming in fast.

I hate this guy. I turned my body into stone to brace for the impact and badly cracked the floor when I made contact. Although the air hadn't fled my lungs, my back and ribs were burning with pain. I squeezed the shaft of my axe. V'rossar dove down. The axe rapidly changed, lengthening into a war hammer. I rolled onto my feet and whirled, swinging the five-foot long shaft upwards. The rectangular head struck him solidly in the jaw, knocking him out of the air. The ground beneath me crunched.

Shaking himself like a bat, he stood on his feet. He spat out some black ichor.

"Not bad," he said, wiping his mouth. "What did you do to yourself? Where did that easily soft skin go? That's too bad, I was actually enjoying myself. I love this stone look, though. What an interesting specimen I have here, wouldn't you say?" he smiled.

"Shut up," I growled.

"How rude!" he spat, his tail darted forward, the crown of barbs flying towards me to skewer me. The war hammer lengthened into a pike. I pointed the spearhead and blocked the barb's thrust.

"Pitiful," he sighed, bored as he coiled his entire tail around my spear. "AGHHHH!" he screamed as sapphire spikes stabbed through his tail.

He tried yanking his tail back; however, the spear wouldn't release him from its barbed embrace. Giant green and lavender purple explosions blossomed where An-u and

Vaughn-ness were. I pulled the spear back and it unfurled V'rossar's tail. The sudden release dropped him to the floor.

"Get up!" I growled.

Unintelligible words flew like arrows from his mouth. My body fell to the ground without my accord and I couldn't move. Another series of words I didn't understand left his mouth. With a flick of his hand, he had me levitating in midair. I tried to move my hand and I couldn't. V'rossar chuckled at my attempts. He bent with his arm extended. His claws wrapped around my throat.

"I was on your trail the moment that you came to this planet," he said, lifting me to the height of his porcupine face. "Your ignorance is quite cute."

My wide eyes and shocked and confused expression gave him cause to laugh feebly.

"Who do you think ordered that pack of dragons to be present moments after your arrival? The dragon that plucked you out of the watered mud basin was acting on my behalf. The fight with the yellow beast, my doing once more. Having you placed in the dragon arena, me again. And then I lost your trail. For seven and a half years I tried to find it. Had Jaow-kieen not taken to the air and gotten back on the grid, so to speak, I would never have found you again," he took a deep breath, smiling in ecstasy.

"How? Why?" I mouthed.

"I have been working towards Maldroto's return for centuries. Since the necromancers of old, now extinct, forged me from the darkest of magics. For five hundred years since my dark birth, I've been gathering the vilest resources and assets to prepare and set about his return. He's my idol, the mission that he had when he landed here all those billions of years ago. His adamant diligence to carry out his cause, the great Crusade. The million-year war campaign that he launched. The resources, tools, warriors, and means that he created, self-made to acquire his goal. It's beyond inspiring. Everything he wanted, he set about. And if he couldn't find it, he invented it. When it came to resourcefulness and industriousness, he was a god."

I was choking on what I was hearing. *If only I could move, damn it!* I cursed.

"I have all I need, except a buffer to bring him back. The scrolls of history and sorcery claim that he's imprisoned in the core of the planet, being subdued by sorcery that no one alive or dead can touch. I've been scouting for abnormalities for thirty decades. When you arrived, my sorcerous radars went off the scales and my legions of sorcerers noticed a slight one percent dip in Maldroto's bonds as well as a simultaneous one percent increase in his strength. I don't know how or why, but you are responsible for this. You have what I need. Within your body lies the key to his return. During the eight years you have been here, his strength has risen to thirty-five percent."

His tail swooped over to me and the sword-length alpha spike hovered over my heart.

"I'm going to harness what you have, to speed up his recovery, so he can break his bonds and return."

Behind him I heard An-u and Vaughn-ness yelling. Dozens of green, purple, and blue explosions were going off. Small dragons were falling out of the air in the hundreds. Hundreds more kept pouring in, replacing them. The smell of burning, incinerated flesh plagued the air. *At least they're holding their own out there.*

"I don't need you alive to use what is in your blood. Now I am going to kill you," he grinned excitedly. "It's been a pleasure meeting you, entertaining you, and thoroughly doing business with you," his face softened into a sympathetic look as my eyes grew wide.

"I'm so sorry," he sweetly batted his eyes.

A lusting, savage grin stretched over his face as he drove the barb forward. It made contact with my chest, right over my heart!

13

Synergetic Impact

Vaughn-ness bounded after An-u, utterly amazed as she combined their sorcery to destroy another horde of V'rossar's dragon fighters. *I haven't seen such strength, skill and hard determination like hers since the war, those last final days,* Vaughn-ness marveled. Vaughn-ness leapt in front of An-u, cutting her off from a spiraling wave of small dragons. He felt a tug in his chest and released a surging avalanche of white fire. The wave of a hundred fighters were incinerated. More ashes rained down. *This guilt! For killing my own! It's a volcano drowning me. But what choice is there? I have none!* Vaughn-ness thought bitterly with sorrow.

"How do you think Zammus is doing? Do you think he's alright?" Vaughn-ness shouted.

An-u ran from behind him, leapt a few inches into the air, and grabbed the legs of two dragons. All of them were about the same size as her. She struck three other dragons down with her makeshift clubs, then swung the bodies of the dragons in her hands and landed on the ground, bashing their skulls on the floor. Purple matter exploded at her feet.

She faced him, "I don't know, Vaughn-ness. I hope he's okay."

She spread her arms wide again as she ran forward into the dragons' ranks. A translucent purple orb the size of a small boulder coalesced above her fingers. She nodded at Vaughn-ness, asking him to add his sorcery. They had been doing this since the fighting started about forty minutes ago. *This is the forty-ninth energy sphere we make,* Vaughn-ness counted as he sliced a trio of dragons with a wing and focused his concentration. A translucent lime green sphere with yellow splotches materialized to the left of him. He bobbed his head towards An-u, directing the sorcerous globe to her.

A swirling vortex of another hundred dragons were spiraling down to attack her. Both spheres of energy hung above her. She slammed her hands together, their sorcery mirroring her gestures. The spheres met in a colliding splash of liquid aqua and bursting violet. The product was a glowing emerald-purple orb twice the size of both. She ran forward to meet the wave of small dragons. She propelled her hands forward and the orb of light was thrown into the swarm. Her fingers clenched into fists. The wave of dragons were all pulled towards the sphere. An-u forcefully opened her hands. The sphere detonated in a blue burst of green and purple light. Scorched and blackened bodies rained down all around them. Though he had seen this spectacle forty-nine times, Vaughn-ness was still awed by her wit and level of mastery.

"Incredible. It's as if she is unstoppable," he whispered.

Two revolving hordes flanked him, jerking him to attention. Vaughn-ness dug his claws into the tiled floor.

"This is beginning to agitate me," he growled.

The twisting wave of a hundred or more dragons on either side of him dove, each releasing small erupting bursts of flame which spun into fireballs.

"A firestorm," Vaughn-ness muttered, recognizing the ancient battle tactic. Two climbing paths of golden white light shot from both of his shoulders, immediately striking the squadrons on each side of him. The airborne hordes on the left and right of him froze as the light ran through their ranks, illuminating each of their bodies all at once and showing their grisly skeletons within. The legions on either side of him collapsed to the ground, their hundreds of bodies shattering. Fire balls painlessly cascaded over Vaughn-ness.

He leapt into the air, pushing his wings open, unsheathing them like swords.

"An-u! How far are we from Jaow-kieen?" he shouted.

She whipped around. "He's there!" she cried, indicating a spiraling black staircase.

Above it, right under the ceiling, sat Jaow-kieen wrapped in his azure spherical prison. Anger bellowed behind Vaughn-ness's eyes as he noticed his dangling, broken arm. He beat his wings and plucked An-u from the ground with his left forepaw.

"We're faster in the air, can cover more distance, and can survey the battle better," he barked, swerving a troop.

Shards of energy leapt from An-u's palm, vaporizing the dragons.

"The enemy will be forced to attack us at this vantage point. It's the only option they'll have and when they launch themselves at us, we'll smoke them out," he communicated, spitting blue fire at a troop diving towards them.

An-u nodded, "They most likely will swarm us all at once. And from what I've seen, aside from trying to kill us, they're completely disorganized, they have no strategy."

She swung her arm in a broad stroke. An arc of blue light was birthed and it swiped into the group ahead of them, hacking dragons and hurling purple viscera and gore with the graceful movement of an axe. With a jerking swing of her arm, she sent the blade of light slicing through the other troops, bending its will to her mind as it severed their enemies in a boomerang fashion. Suddenly a bellowing that mirrored thunderclaps pounded the entire cavern, shaking Vaughn-ness and An-u's concentration.

"Dragons. Big ones!" Vaughn-ness shouted as brutes almost the size of him charged out from hidden battlements and tunnels along the levels. A scarlet beast entirely covered in spines with a keel-shaped jaw leapt off a floor, traveling an improbable one hundred and fifty feet with closed wings. Four other dragons that were bigger jumped from the same floor, following their leader. With their wings tucked into their backs and their forelegs extended they resembled arrows.

"An-u! Get out of here! Get to your father! I'll cover you!" Vaughn-ness roared.

"NO!" An-u cried.

"Go! Now!" he bellowed with anger in his voice.

"We stay together, damn it!" An-u yelled, with an edge and order to her voice that startled and silenced Vaughn-ness.

The five dragons were closing in, as they gained speed with a V-shaped formation.

"This is getting old. Haven't I done enough fighting?" Vaughn-ness whispered. "Destroy the little ones, I'll nullify these," he said with unbroken calm.

His wings began to glow with a blinding white light. He spun through the air, touching each of his five adversaries. As his wings made contact with a dragon it disintegrated into motes of white light. The leader and two of his comrades were taken out. But two dragons; a dark blue and a yellow remained. They charged.

"Those two must be completely fearless or utterly brainless," An-u observed as she loosed an arrow into the eye of the yellow one. The dragon careened, shrieking, dragging An-u along. The blue brute slammed into Vaughn-ness, swiping at his throat with its overly long jaws.

"You fool. Fighting for the wrong cause," Vaughn-ness sighed, back-handing the dragon with a paw.

The beast instantly dissolved into pinpricks of light and ash. Vaughn-ness spotted An-u below, struggling to sprint up a winding black staircase as she was bombarded by a spiraling formation of what had to be over five hundred small dragons. Three large dragons–an orange, copper-and-white, and mottled black–were also picking at her, breathing streams of fire, completely unconcerned that they were also destroying their smaller troops. An oval-shaped sphere of golden light surrounded her. Whenever a dragon touched it, it would burst in a spray of blood. She was beginning to tire; twice her shield flickered and vanished. The three large dragons moved as one, each striking the sorcerous shield with an unrelenting trail of white fire propelled from angry jaws.

A tentacle of golden light struck out from within the shield. The tendril slammed the black-and-white dragon, constricted around it, and squeezed. Its body further blackened as the tentacle continued tightening. The dragon burst into red crisps and black ashes. Vaughn-ness fwirled over to her in an eruption of sapphire light. He thrust the claws of his left paw into the air, making a wicked gesture. All of the dragons encircling them, colossal and small, collapsed falling forward, purple blood bursting from their jaws, their torsos ripped apart from within as their hearts exploded. An-u's golden shield came down as she stood gaping.

"Come on, we need to move," Vaughn-ness urged, looking up at Jaow-kieen's azure prison.

Knowing what he had in mind, she jumped into his paw. He nodded as blue energy wrapped around them. Jaow-kieen's sapphire prison materialized before them.

"You should not have come, daughter. Grand master, it can't be you. It is beyond possible. You don't exist anymore!" Jaow-kieen muttered, limping around the enormous orb of his prison.

"Father! You're hurt!" An-u sniffled a sob as she laid eyes upon his right arm.

It was broken in two places: at the wrist, and at the juncture of elbow and bicep. There was a gaping hole in the center of his forearm that was oozing an emerald-green pus. She also beheld his bonds, ropes of opaque purple light that encased his paws and a purple-green orb that engulfed his jaws. She gasped, tears coming to her eyes as she watched him hobble around, his infected limb tucked into an accustomed bent position as it dangled.

"Where's Zammus?" Jaow-kieen coughed, his golden bronze eyes possessing a deranged look.

"He's here," she answered.

"An-u, defend and cover us. I have to break these complex and ancient bonding spells that are holding him.

Hold them off for five minutes. That is all it will take," Vaughn-ness ordered.

"Right."

Insanely deep tones and guttural growls crawled out of Vaughn-ness's throat as red, purple and yellow sparks began flickering around him and over Jaow-kieen's prison. An enormous brown dragon, leading a mixed legion of large and small beasts slammed right into An-u.

***

The barb got no further than gently touching the stone of my skin. The spear flew out of my immobilized hand and rapidly flickered into a cantaloupe-sized sphere that was blinking blue and white. My eyes gleamed, growing wide with utter fear. The flashing orb hurled itself into V'rossar's voluminous black cloak, distracting him enough to release his strangling and sorcerous grip on me. I fell to the ground. His body collapsed as it twisted into a thick black substance. He now resembled a smoky curtain-like mist. However, his head remained.

The orb, flickering white and blue, was throbbing from within the center of his inky, murky form. His eyes grew wider than spoons as he shrieked, "It doesn't matter what happens to me! He's still coming back! He is imprisoned right beneath us! Why do you think I erected this fortress right here! There's not a thing you can do! He will return regardless of what you think! Hail Lord Maldroto! He will return! Hail!"

He was cut off as hundreds of sapphire rays sliced out of him, bursting him. I shoved my head into my forearms, burying my face and pressing my body as low to the ground as possible. As inconceivable heat blazed and infinite blue light raged through my eyelids.

***

The hordes of their assailants stopped their relentless attack. Thousands of slitted eyes froze as they were captivated by a titanic erupting wave of blue energy that had started from the center of the vast chamber and was spreading, bellowing out. The legion assaulting An-u halted, every action ceased. The leader, a brown bulk of a dragon, was caught midway in striking another blow to An-u, the muscles in his thick tail coiled to strike, the barb on its tip poised to stab, his right forearm locked, gray talons hooked inches from An-u's face.

"They all stopped, Vaughn-ness! What's going on?" she shouted, as she turned to face him.

"Finished!" he exclaimed victoriously as Jaow-kieen's cell and shackles dissolved into pink mist. "An-u, what was that you said?" Vaughn-ness asked, as he draped a protective wing over his adopted grandson.

By then An-u had already answered her own question. Like all of the hundreds of reptilian statues around her, she was staring at the burst of sapphire energy that mirrored the force of a volcanic eruption. It was a dome of immeasurable proportion that was ablaze with azure-blue streaks and crackling white bolts of energy. The eruption of energy had reached the height of the ceiling and was spreading out horizontally in sky-blue shockwaves.

"Zammus!" An-u cried, already knowing.

"Oh my," Jaow-kieen answered.

"Oh my indeed," Vaughn-ness breathed.

"Father!" An-u screamed, running over to Jaow-kieen and laying her cheek on his broken arm.

"An-u, you know that we can't save him. We would if we could, but we have no time," he croaked with emotion.

The cavern shuddered horrendously. Pillars crashed, shattering to the floor. Levels and balconies caved in and elaborate masonry pulsed and cracked, splitting like vicious ice. Enormous, savage, and jagged cracks angrily broke out of the floors, lining their surfaces with bold black veins. Thousands of frightened roars, growls, and yelps struck the air like a harp note as V'rossar's forces took to the air, massacring its softness in an attempt to save themselves.

"We can't stay here," Vaughn-ness spoke gravely, hating himself with every word.

The shockwaves of energy were expanding at a rate that seemed to be quickly accelerating with each beat of his heart. Everything they touched was obliterated in a sea of blue flames and white lightning.

"I'm sorry, Zammus. I really am," Vaughn-ness moaned, sobbing as light pink and blue fluid ran from his eyes and nostrils.

The dragons above were flying haphazardly, completely out of control as they careened into each other, accidentally knocking each other out of the air and crashing into broken masonry.

"Wow, V'rossar took away their ability to fwirl. That's why they are acting so hysterical. They can't escape. They really were his slaves," Jaow-kieen observed, remarking to himself.

"We have to go now! It's now or never!" Vaughn-ness yelled, tears leaping from his eyes as he tore through the air with his claws, slicing open a portal.

On the other side lay a green forest made of jade that housed pink, purple, and blue krystal flowers. The tremors shaking the fortress doubled in strength, tearing aggressive cracks in the walls as they were split from floor to ceiling. Gaping craters were consuming the floor and bronze ceiling. Masonry began raining down in large dragon and boulder-sized chunks.

"Zammus! I am beyond sorry for having brought you into this. The guilt of your death will eternally be on my wings!" Jaow-kieen wept.

"Zammus!" An-u cried, tears rapid and rabid, biting and stinging her eyes and cheeks.

"We'll come back for him!" Vaughn-ness affirmed.

"I promise!" Jaow-kieen swore.

The blue waves were crackling and swarming above them.

"There won't be anything left of him!" An-u squealed, biting down on her lip painfully.

"We have to try," Jaow-kieen soothed.

"We have to, and we will," Vaughn-ness mirrored. "And we can only do that if we are alive."

"ZAMMUS!" An-u yelled sobbing through heavy tears.

"We will return! I PROMISE! We all PROMISE!" they cried as one.

Vaughn-ness pushed all three of them into the portal with a swoop of his wing just as forking spears of blue energy and white hammering swords of lightning destroyed the last part of the fortress Onoguol. On the other side of the portal in the krystal-flowered forest, they watched as relentless titanic energy engulfed where they had just been. Vaughn-ness closed the portal. An-u fell to the ground, Vaughn-ness's and

Jaow-kieen's heads thumping heavily beside her. All three cried fully and very openly.

14

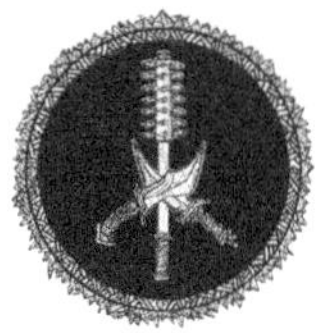

Explosion Event

The woman crouched, intent as she studied the paw prints before her. She had pale gray skin and jet-black hair that was fastened into a thick braid that fell to the small of her back. She was clad in a copper-colored lightly armored jerkin that showed off her powerfully lean, toned, and chiseled arms. Shorts of the same color and make clothed her legs, ending at mid-thigh. Greaves and vambraces, the color of red-orangish clay and made of light stone, covered her shins and forearms. The shaft of a large dagger protruded from between the greave of her left leg. Her feet were bare. Strapped onto her back was a long mace.

She didn't at all look her age; where she came from no one did. Everyone stopped physically aging in their mid-twenties and thirties, their prime. She was still considered young in the minds of her people, having breathed for one hundred and thirty-three years. She dipped the fingers of her right hand into the strange paw print. They were fresh. After a moment or so she withdrew her fingers and restored a pair of brown padded fingerless gloves over her hands. She stood up as a violent tremor shuddered the ground. Her bright orange and fierce green eyes blazed, gaping in bewilderment and curious shock. Her gaze was focused on a growing burst of light about a mile away.

As blue light erupted across the landscape, glowing blue shockwaves of energy were racing across the vast plain, relentlessly blazing in her direction, dissolving as they got closer and closer, losing force, strength and substance as the waves withered into smoky, faded, stringy, phantom-like wisps that were shortly preyed upon and swallowed by the wind. Another titanic tremor wrestled with the earth, this time throwing the woman off her feet. She narrowed her eyes, gasping as she made out the surging mass of light that was so far away.

"That's the old fortress," she breathed as she pinpointed the source. She slowly got to her feet, standing at five feet and five inches. "I have to abandon the search, the hunt, my tracking. This new set of events has stolen my interest. So now I must investigate."

The woman slid the large dagger into her hand and with her other hand plucked her mace from over her back. Armed, she began making her way at a brisk steady walk over to the pulsating and spasming blue light.

15

Resolution, Wielding Pretense

I was paralyzed and cold. Not only physically, but mentally and emotionally as well. Physically I was perfectly intact; that I knew. Nothing had impacted me. I slowly opened my eyes for the dozenth time knowing what I would find. A translucent glass-like sphere of light surrounding me. Beyond their protective walls was oblivion. What was Onoguol? An-u, Vaughn-ness, Jaow-kieen, and I would know. It had been wiped off the face of existence. There was nothing left. Utterly nothing. Empires of toppled, broken, cracked stone were littered all around me. Legions of mountains and hillocks of pulverized stone towered above me in all directions. I shakily uncurled myself from the wound-up fetal position that I had held for who knows how long.

Trembling with every fiber of my being, I got to my feet. *Why had the staff done this?* I thought, equally bitter and mortified.

None of this was necessary. The staff could have just killed V'rossar in a small and simple explosion. What had it been trying to prove? Was it still trying to prove something? And if so, what was it and more importantly, why?

The blue walls around me pulsed patiently. I needed to get out of this grave. I looked around once more. As if reading my thoughts, the spherical walls flared outward and with a shimmering *pop!* that made the light dance at the corners of my eyes, the blue mass had coalesced into a dull and unassuming sapphire broadsword. Directly above my head, just an arm's reach away, infinite layers of stone and debris shifted in this new pocket of air, no longer being held back by the staff's shield. My heart pulsed in my mouth and another azure glowing sphere blossomed into being, totally engulfing me. Detritus harmlessly battered the shield, crunching and disintegrating on impact. Closing my eyes and sighing I breathed again.

"Let's please not do that again!" I wheezed. Despite its protection, I wanted nothing to do with the staff right now after all it had done. "Where are the others? An-u, Jaow-kieen, Vaughn-ness?" I croaked, swallowing the lump of emotion in my throat.

A turquoise, aqua-colored sphere a meter in diameter materialized above the sword, blooming into being. White light swam, flowing within it like milk. Images ignited, sprouting into focus. Sound exploded around me, bursting in titanic volumes. A scene flared into existence. I saw Vaughn-ness, An-u, and Jaow-kieen as if they were right in front of me. Oceans of exploding, blue light were swarming, closing in around them, rolling in tsunami-sized waves. All three were huddled up, Vaughn-ness in the middle with An-u and Jaow-kieen on either side of him, the green mountains of his wings clasping them to him.

"We have to go now! It's now or never!" he roared, tears flying from his eyes as he swiped with his arm, talons cutting through the air. A landscape revealed itself through the fissure. It was earth green and populated by flowers that had to have been cut from rainbow-colored glass and grown by sorcery.

"ZAMMUS!" An-u wailed, with such a high note and pitch that her cry sliced through my body.

Bright sapphire blue tears clung to her face like jewels. Her dark yet radiant eyes looked pained, like a raging, blustering storm illumined with clashing lightning.

"We have to try!" Jaow-kieen coughed, tears the color of molten gold running down his snout.

The space holding them collapsed to half its size as aggressive crackling blue energy poured downward, diving inward. Vaughn-ness's purple and blue eyes flashed. The blue tempest crackled, blue and white tendrils of energy feeling curiously and eagerly reaching, only inches from their flesh.

"ZAMMUS! We will return! I promise! We all promise!" They yelled together.

As one they leapt into the portal, Vaughn-ness pulling them with him. Through the portal on the other side, I saw them and the dark burdensome storm clouds of their guilt hanging over them. The portal immediately blinked out like a great eye. The raging torrent of blue and white persisted, destroying and washing out what little remained. The orb hovering above the sword burst like a water droplet, its sorcerous essence reconnecting with the sword as it flowed into it. I had regained the will to move forward.

"Thank you for showing me that. I needed to see," I said.

The broadsword glowed momentarily, before dimming once more.

"Let's move. We've stayed here long enough," I spoke.

Where? I asked my mind.

"I don't know." I said.

Will I ever see them again? my mind inquired.

"I don't know."

I reached within my body, myself. Spikes of stone and obsidian grew out of me like fresh shoots. My body rippled with thickness, elongation, and armor. *Oh, the power of stone!* I relished.

"How do we get out of here?" I asked myself, eyeing the endless towering destruction.

The sword erupted into a rippling sheet and poured itself into the walls around me, adding to the sphere. Having reinforced the layers of the protective bubble, the staff sped us away, racing upwards and obliterating debris as it smashed through them, rendering and reducing them to motes of light. In moments we were free from the wreckage and on bare sandy ground. Three suns–two dark orange, and one yellow–were shining down, marking the late afternoon. The orb dissolved around me and rematerialized as a barely noticeable, fingernail-thin blue thread that looped around one of the long, ragged spikes on my armored forearm, completely out of sight.

I looked around me; no one and nothing was afoot. Once again, I was awed and, yes, frightened. Not as much as before, but still by what the staff had caused. The sheer level and magnitude of utter destruction. Never having seen the outside of the fortress of Onoguol, I could not compare it in its destruction. It looked like a colossal mammoth of a black mountain had collapsed and been split and sliced up by vengeful and rampaging plate tectonics. From the outside it was impossible to be aware of the devastated subterraneous levels that spanned from several hundred to a thousand feet deep below.

I took a deep breath. "Enough sightseeing. Let's go," I said to myself.

With that I started at a moderate gallop running parallel to the destruction, which I assume must have been visible for miles around. All the while I thought about the staff.

I don't understand the staff. It has saved and protected me for the most part; it is a hand-me-down from Jaow-kieen, yet didn't at all protect me from a dragon; completely destroys Onoguol, forcibly separates the others from me, yet helps me and continues to do so without asking for a price. It has never asked. Maybe perhaps one day it will ask for an impossible or inconceivable one to pay up for all it has done. I do owe it without end. Whose side is it on? What if it's an anura?! But that wouldn't be possible! Couldn't! Can't. An-u's the last one. The others were all destroyed. Or were they? Jaow-kieen said. He would know, more and better than I ever could. Why am I here and not with them? Perhaps by isolating me, the staff believes that I can grow and develop more for my role, be self-autonomous, and discover my necessary strength and prowess. Or the staff could be leading towards the complete opposite. Don't trust it. That is completely contradictory. I have no choice. Trust fate. Regardless of all that has happened, trust fate. I have to. I am supposed to be here. I was supposed to come to this planet and into these circumstances. Fate decreed it. Trust fate, Zammus. I have no choice. I have to, I concluded.

"Enough reflections," I said.

I slowed to a brief trot and stopped.

A woman stood in front of me, five to ten yards away.

Where'd she come from? Don't tell me that I was that engrossed in thought that I completely failed to notice her. What a disaster of awareness! She didn't just spring up! I stared, shocked and very much irate at my obliviousness.

She was entirely made of gray stone; her flesh was the color of granite. I stood still, both stunned, surprised, and completely wary.

Let her approach. She comes to you, you have the upper ground, I thought.

I was completely curious though, never having seen a creature of stone aside from myself. She looked incredibly marvelous and beyond beautiful with jet-black hair that was braided to her back, the tip swaying from side to side as it was breathed on by the wind. She was clothed in copper-colored armor that covered her thighs and torso, but not her upper arms. Padded armor the color of papayas adorned her forearms and heavily muscled, thick and sculpted lower shins. Her feet were completely exposed. From this distance I could see her black obsidian toes and fingernails. Each foot and hand ended in five digits.

Her hands were garbed in a brown material that exposed her fingers and deeply resembled leather. Within those hands lay savage weapons. In her right hand was a long, spiked dagger the length of her forearm and hand included. Within her left was a four-sided mace with smooth, long spikes. The entire weapon was the length of her torso, neck, and head combined. Her eyes were glowing, peering into me. Each eye was a blazing mixture of bright orange and lime green, with an orange sclera and green iris. They were interesting, unsettling, feral, calm, war-like, experienced, wise, hard, battle-hardened, intelligent and complex, lovely and beautiful all at the same time.

Her striking gaze punched me, shooting through the exterior of the beast and into the man within. The silence was long, pervading like a blade without end. For five minutes it stabbed the air, piercing through its seams. The woman's eyes never blinked.

"I have been hunting you. Creature. Beast," she finally spoke.

I nodded at her philosophically, trying to display a competent intelligence. I squinted my great blue eyes, faked a yawn, aimlessly wagged my tail and flicked an ear. Trying to appear quite daft, dumb, and bored.

Hunting me? How did you know I even exist? Then it hit me like an anvil. *My tracks! The likes of them had never been seen before!*

I growled out a groan and grunted a sigh. I gazed at the ground, intent on a six-digit paw print. My gaze returned to her and I slowly began walking over. She didn't retreat or lower her weapons. I stopped two yards from her, towering over her by a good ten to twelve feet. Her gaze was relentless, but intensely curious.

"I have been tracking you since I spotted a strange pair of tracks east of the Imperengú River some weeks past. Alongside its edge for miles I spotted two pairs of tracks. It was obvious that one belonged to a dragon, the other clearly to a creature unknown. For weeks I lost your trail once they vanished into the heart of an emerald krystal forest," she chattered in the way that people address animals.

Weeks?! How can that be?! That was just yesterday . . . I swallowed, uneasy. *Time moves so strangely here. So . . . imperceptibly . . . fast. What felt like a few weeks with*

Jaow-kieen was actually eight years. So I was told. But how? Not now, I redirected my thoughts.

So how then did you get back on my trail? I questioned, trying to focus on the here and now. *When Grath had fwirled us to Onoguol he could have taken us anywhere, on the other side of the planet for all I knew. Or a day's walk from where we had fought. Something was going on. Inevitably there was something amiss. This woman knows about it,* I reasoned, rationalizing immaterial puzzle pieces.

Wind swirled over her features, licked the spines covering my body, and swirled the pale orange sand into clouds. Despite her relentless stare, fancy weapons, and rugged appearance, she was all showmanship. She had no magic about her; this I was able to gauge by how she carried herself. Strikingly confident and very intimidating as she was, sorcery was not reflected in her composure. She would have used it and displayed her dominance already, not study me and talk. I had the upper hand here and she knew it. This would go my way, however and whichever way I chose it. I could ignore her, run off, and go my own way; or consent to whatever her wishes may be, which most likely included following her and letting her lead me to wherever she came from. And of course, what she instinctively feared was me attacking and severely harming her.

I will go with her. She strikes me as curious and this is an opportunity that can provide me with insight, knowledge and experience, I decided.

Looking even deeper into her face I moved my left paw. Drawn to the movement her eyes darted to the ground. Sliding my claws through the dirt as if I had palsy and delayed mental functioning, and severely low intelligence as many individuals assumably expect animals to have, I scrawled something. The woman's weapons clattered to the ground as she backed away, gasping and shaking, her eyes glued to the ground. In sloppy dashes it spelled out *LEAD*.

16

Duplicitous Farce; A New Role To Play

I wondered what I was doing. Another part of me told me to just go with it and see where it goes. *You're deceiving her! Letting her think you are this beastly creature,* my mind spat.

No. Well . . . I am this creature. It's an aspect of me, a part. She just doesn't know the rest, I thought.

Still deceit! my mind shot back.

I didn't reply, having nothing to say and not having the energy to argue rationally. For hours we walked, covering who knows how many miles and unknown lands. Over deserts, through canyons, across magma streams, within empty and ash gray valleys. She was a relentless hiker.

Where does she come from? I pondered as we met our first mountains.

The terrain had become dryer and more arid as we had continued. I hadn't seen a body of lava for what felt like two or three hours. My tongue was swollen and my shoulders had a slight ache and sag to them. For a time I couldn't calculate I had seen only two types of land: desert and earth, cracked like broken glass and dehydrated wrinkles. The latter was the type that was currently under our feet. Above us the mountains were an onyx black, not that tall or formidable. I closely watched the woman as she gazed at the mountains, assessing their peaks. She drew her mace and lightly tapped a ridge of rock in front of her. A light *tink!* filled the air. An orange and desert-brown pole reached out of the ground, growing until it stopped at the height of her thigh.

An opening slowly revealed itself at the base of the mountain. Broken steps retreated into the darkness. I squinted in confusion.

She turned to me, "This is where we rest. Tomorrow, we resume at dawn."

I looked around. The orange sky was slowly being consumed by purple rays. Aside from her, I hadn't seen another life form all day. Four light blue crescent moons were seated at each of the four corners of the sky. The woman disappeared down the steps, consumed by utter darkness. I didn't want to go down there.

Yet every step I have taken since I've been on this planet has been a leap without certainty, I said to myself.

So into the dark I followed her. With a roar that made me growl in fear and shock, the mountain shook and shuddered as the opening closed. Bright red and orange light illuminated our surroundings. Lava was flowing all over the walls just like the cavern where I had first met Vaughn-ness. Pools of magma littered the ground.

"Here's food and sustenance," the woman gestured.

She hunkered down into a squat and dipped her hands into a pool in front of her and brought them to her lips, the life of fire dripping down her chin. I brought my head to the nearest bowl of lava and greedily drank. After the woman and I had our fill, we each retired and turned into ourselves, she sitting with her back against the wall opposite me, her weapons laid before her feet, inches from her grasp. I laid down, stretching myself beside the wall facing her. We looked at each other momentarily. Woman and beast. Actually, the man within. Her blank stare matched my exhausted one.

My brain slowed as memories resurfaced. Like a swirling tide, my past flowed into me. Images of the life I had had thrust into me like a tsunami. *When I used to be human. Just human. Nothing else. What I had been. The principal navigator of the* Mantis. *A fiancé. Valaura. An older brother. My crew. Whatever happened to the last two people I ever saw? Deemetri and old pelican-haired Parce? In the treasure hoard where I had found it before I touched it. The anura. Are they even alive? What year is it back home in Britain? How is Valaura dealing with my absence? Has she married someone else? Probably. Most definitely! How is William Withersby Suel, my adopted little brother? They all must think I abandoned them or I'm dead.*

None of this matters anymore. Your past. What was. You don't have a home anymore. This is the reality. My reality. Caused by the greed of your own nature, the greed of men. Of human nature. All because of some stupid treasure and jewels. It's irreversible. I never wanted this. How could I have known . . . I never wanted this.

My eyes rolled over as I regarded my giant spike-covered stone paws, the white stone and black obsidian glimmering under my gaze. I got up and paced, wondering what on earth I was doing and doing here. I imagine something was consuming the woman and eating her up pretty well too; though tired as she seemed, she refused to close her eyes.

Show her what you are, I thought.

No. It's not time. There is still so much to witness from this vantage point. Show all your cards and she'll have leverage over you, I fought back.

Patience, my mind argued.

All the while as my thoughts battled each other she watched me, her face calm as stone, and weary, yet at the same time in those features there was an unwavering sense of sharpness and discernment akin to a peregrine falcon. I laid down once again facing her and tried to sleep.

I hope the past lets me, I thought.

***

I woke to find the woman standing up and strapping on her weapons. My evening wish had been granted; the memories of the past had abided. But I had been molested by fearful, paralyzing phantasms of the future. I rose to my limbs and flicked my snout in the direction of the woman. In return she briefly surveyed me with her eyes. I made my way over to the nearest lava pit and drank for a few moments. I raised my head, ready to go. She led the way as we walked through the cavern, streams of lava eternally gliding over the walls in glowing ripples like liquid gold. She stopped in front of a wall, drew her mace, and placed its tip against the rock.

How did she remember the exact spot? All the walls look the same, I wondered. Just as before the wall opened up and sunlight poured in like water, drowning us in its rays.

The landscape changed as we continued. Purple flowers of spiraling krystal dominated the ground, which was fed by a plentitude of lava marshes and streams. The ground itself was moist with lava it couldn't hold back. Small droplets peppered every inch of its surface. Surrounding us were towering black and gray jagged ridges that appeared to vanish into the sky. Strange creatures roamed these lands. Stocky rhinoceros-sized beasts that were colored gray like their African counterparts but made of stone and shaped completely differently. The best that I can describe them is that they were giant stone pangolins. They roamed in peaceful slow-moving herds as they lapped up lava with glowing blue tongues, played, watched their frolicking cubs, and slept. They paid us very little attention as we walked through their lands.

"These are parfins, Beast," the woman said suddenly, her first words to me all day. "Back home they are our steeds and companions for life. They are loyal to their kin and companions for life."

Intrigued, I nodded.

The parfins regarded me with gentle purple, green, and blue eyes. A violent flash of purple-yellow light struck down before the woman and I, throwing us apart. Yellow-gray smoke filled the air and as it cleared four figures came into view. Three prugalas and a navy-blue medium-sized dragon about the size of a five-carriage supply train, some twenty-five to forty feet in length.

"Murgen!" the tallest and thickest prugala called with open arms. "How nice to see you! Thought we'd never see you again! We tracked and tracked and tracked you all to no avail. Ain't that right, fellas?"

There were calls, cries, and hoots of agreement and shouts of "Murgen!"

"Buzz off, Shenrai, I left the group years ago," the woman, Murgen, said.

"I can't. You know our oaths, the ways of our code and doctrine. Dishonor by desertion is death," the prugala said, a grin slowly creeping over his face.

Like him, the other two prugalas were dressed in tattered and stringy cloaks and fitted breeches. Above their eye ridges were goggles fashioned from some kind of rock. They each carried a tan-colored staff. The dragon was the most bizarre and largest oddity of the group. On each limb at its elbows and knees was strapped a black obsidian disc at least the size of a dinghy. On each of its shoulders was a sleek pyramid-shaped apparatus and a spherical helmet that covered the entirety of its head with the exception of its orange eyes and five ash-gray horns.

What on earth is this and what ridiculousness is it wearing? I thought.

"What is that ugly wretched thing at your side?" the dragon spat at Murgen.

"Gruesome beastie! Hurts my eyes!" one of the smaller prugalas cried, launching brown phlegm at my feet.

"Doesn't matter," the leader, Shenrai said. "They're both going to be dead very soon. Vluthe!" He signaled to the dragon.

Blue patches of light gathered at the tips of the pyramids on its shoulders. In less than a blink, blue waves of heat and chaos erupted from their points in a straight line. I swallowed Murgen in a tangle of my limbs, clutching her to my chest as I rolled into a ball, spinning to dodge the reach of the beams. A bellowing thunderclap shook the landscape. *Those are cannons!* I realized, shaking with inconceivable fear.

"Don't let that thing escape!" I heard someone yell.

I unfurled myself, pinning Murgen to my chest with one arm. The three prugalas surrounded us.

"Square them!" Shenrai ordered.

Each of them flexed their fingers and in turn, the sand shivered under my feet as four solid walls were birthed and willed by the manipulation of the infinite grains, as one the walls simultaneously grew in height and began closing in around us.

There's no time to think. You know what you have to do, I thought.

"Stop this madness, Shenrai! This isn't necessary!" Murgen screamed.

"This couldn't be more necessary!" he yelled back.

The walls shimmered as hardened spikes of sand about a yard long grew out of them.

"Vluthe! Now!" Shenrai commanded.

The dragon was hovering above the wall, blue light coalescing in its cannons. In a flash of thought, I was standing on two legs in a man-shaped body made of stone, my staff in hand. The staff split in two. A sphere of its essence engulfed Murgen and I, and the other half, in the form of a sledgehammer, sped toward the dragon as blue light was discharged from its weapons. The sapphire hammer was lost in the blue tide of light. The air rippled fiercely as the hammer tore through the dragon's cannons. There was no erupting flash of light, just a translucent, but clearly visible, discharged sphere of air that dropped the beast out of the air in a detonating thunderclap.

The hammer was back in my hand and the sphere engulfing the two of us collapsed into the hammer, enlarging its head and shaft.

"Let's go!" I barked at her shocked, paralyzed, and confused face.

I threw the hammer at the closest wall, shattering it. The others came down dissolving into sand.

"Where are they?" Murgen gasped, her weapons drawn.

"Here!" a voice yelled from the left.

We turned.

"Not there, there!" the high-pitched voice toyed. "Under you!" The voice hissed as the ground lurched, squeezing and tightening around my feet like quicksand.

Two shapes burst from beneath me in an eruption of sand. The prugalas knocked me to the ground, throwing me on my back. Pinning my arms down, they spread them and covered them with thick manacles of earth that were anchored to the ground by means beyond my mind's comprehension.

"We can kill you right now, Rockhead!" the prugala on my right hissed.

"How about now?" his companion on my left suggested as he willed a torso-sized, anvil-shaped block of sand to hover above me. I looked for Murgen and found her laying on her back, kicking and screaming in midair. I jerked and shook my arms. My captors laughed shrilly and rewarded me by spitting on my face. From the corner of my vision I observed the blue dragon was back on its feet.

Its shoulders were dripping with purple blood, black and gray shrapnel was all that was left of its cannons. Now I saw the functionality of the discs on its limbs and its helmet. Purple rings of energy were pouring out from them as they radiated and kept Murgen afloat. *What type of equipment or tools are those? How can this world possess such means? That is a levitational apparatus! How can that be?* I questioned, realizing I knew absolutely nothing about this world or its inhabitants.

The End
of Volume One of Book One
of
The Anura Chronicles

A note on cliffhangers

Cliffhangers are just insufferable, I know. I can't stand them! No one can, frankly. And I never would have imagined that I would leave anyone, least of all you, dear reader on such a precipitous hang! Especially in the middle of a battle. Heavens forbid! Please don't hurl infinitum expletives at me!

I do assure you however, that this is the only cliff-hanger in the entire set of volumes. And can promise to an absolute T that Volumes 2-4 will include a "Here's the story so far" catch-up section at the beginning of each so no one will have to play any unwanted guess work.

Please forgive me, this cliffhanger wasn't done on purpose!

See you shortly in Volume 2!

Your patience is much appreciated, I guarantee the wait won't be long.

Much obliged.

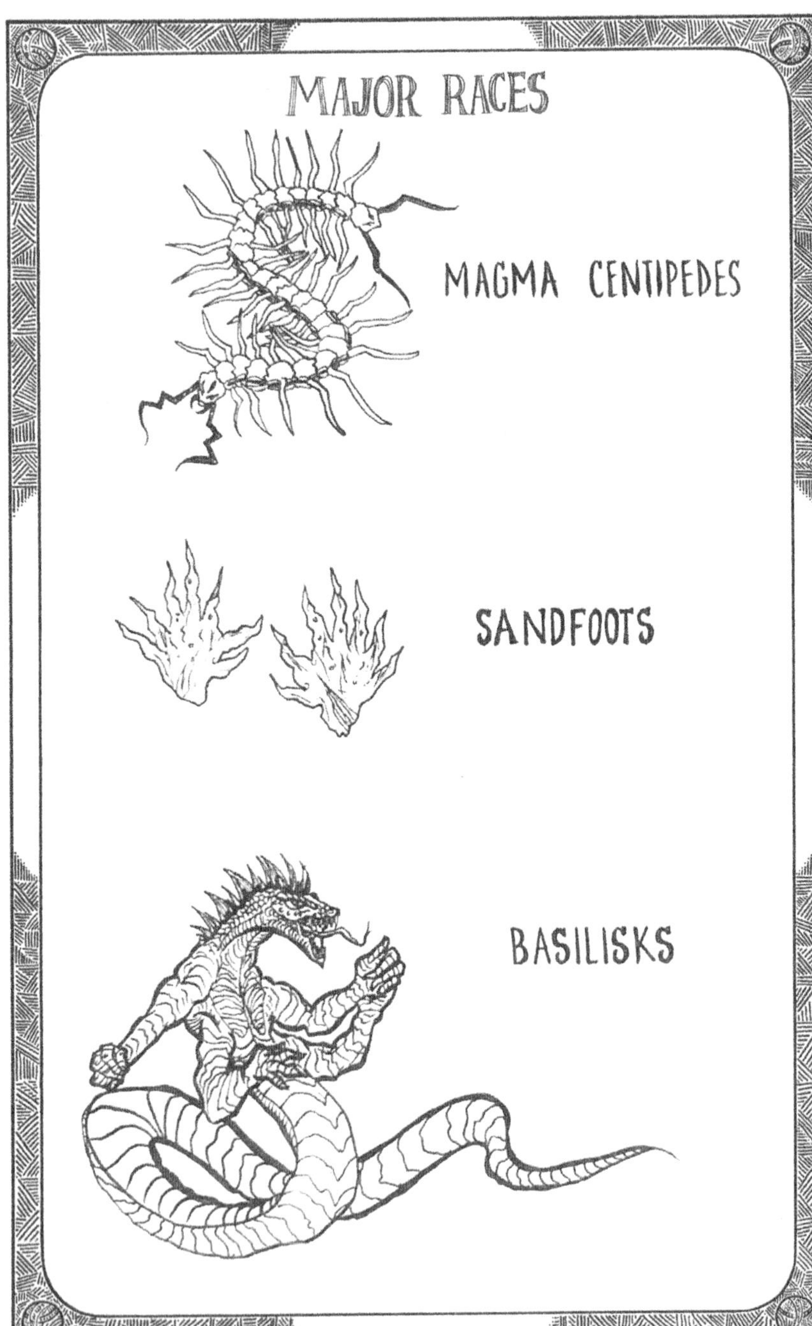
MAJOR RACES
MAGMA CENTIPEDES
SANDFOOTS
BASILISKS

MAJOR RACES

PRUGALAS

DRAGONS

MAJOR RACES

AURÍLS

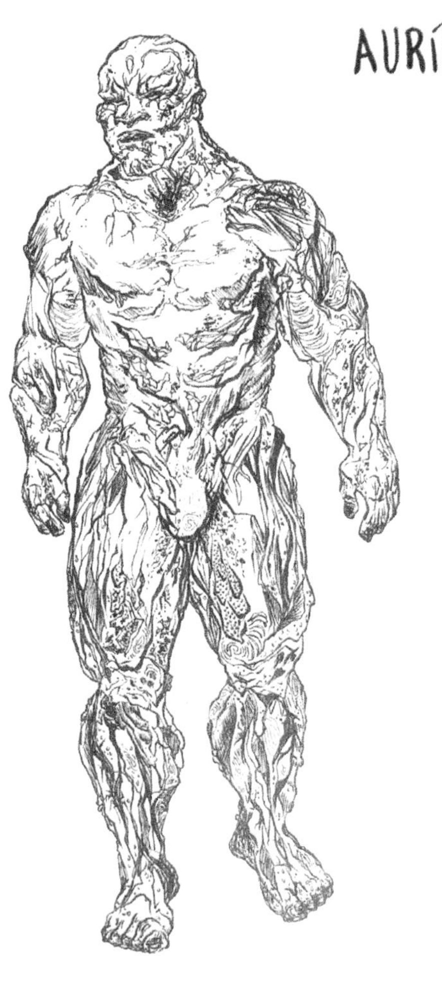

Name pronunciation guide

An-u: On-New

Anura: Anne-your-ah

Aråb-Duele: Air-rub-dool (rhymes with tool)

Dar Vagoue: Dar (rhymes with car) Vog (rhymes with log) u. Dar-vog-u

Jaow-kieen: Jh-ao (ao pronounced as ow) Keen (rhymes with spleen) Jh-ao-Keen

Maldroto: Mall (rhymes with wall) Drot (rhymes with knot) Toe. Mall-drot-toe

Murgen: Mur (rhymes with purr) Gen (rhymes with men)

Shárohlas: Shar (rhymes with bar) Oh-las

Vaughn-ness: Von (rhymes with dawn) Ness. Von-ness

Vreishri' Gaael: Ver (rhymes with fair) Rish (rhymes with wish) Rye. Guy-el. Ver-rish-rye-guy-el

Yvylara: Yv (rhymes with give) Ylara (the second y is silent) Lara. Yv-el-lara

Zammus Dre' Suel: Zam-mus Dray Sool (rhymes with pool)

Dictionary

Fwirl

Noun and verb.

\ fuh-whirl

Fwirl, fwirled, fwirling, fwirlation.

Usage: the suffix form, fwirlation is not particularly used or observed in speaking conventions. Fwirl is more commonly utilized instead as a noun or verb.

The phenomenon and innate ability for a dragon to vibrate and rattle their scales at such high oscillating speeds that allows them to disappear and reappear from one plane of reality to another instantaneously in an eruption of light. Physically moving through space, between two points while rapidly, imperceptibly traversing the distance between the two.

*Limitations: a dragon cannot fwirl to a destination/location that it has not been to before. Fwirling is only possible through memory recall.

*Fwirlation is not teleportation. Though they are similar, but not the same. Teleportation involves closing the distance between two points in space without closing the gap between the two. Whereas with fwirling, the distance between point A and B is in fact is being traveled, just at a velocity that the eye cannot measure.

Goshii

Noun.

\ go-shee

An exercise apparatus that specializes in bodyweight movements. It comprises of cables or long ribbons and a large pair of rings you place your hands in to balance. Think about gymnastic rings.

Sorcery vocabulary glossary

*Different races have different words, phrases and vocabulary for casting spells and commands. Not all sorceries and magic systems are the same or universal. There are varied sorcerous practices, methodologies, instruction, applications and origins spanning geography, culture and race.

Sorcerous phrases practiced by dragons and An-u

Arabula Moêr!
Meaning; Make fire! Or a variant translation; Give life to flame!

Ash Ârí zelsus!
Meaning; Sheath those thighs!

Bluribula Ingulftias.
Meaning; Protect us from this rain.

Goshii Oüshîn Wutâ iesin Shâtá!
Meaning; Goshii and the small structures holding you ascend to me!

Oulaura Vöcis!
Meaning; Become limp! Or a variant translation; Loosen!

Shusara vílm rö vâ Dräk!
Meaning; Collapse in on yourself and reduce to a pebble!

Languages and phrases

Prugala culture

Nawga

The direct translation means "not a." Its broader cultural context and meaning literally translates as "not of scale" i.e. scaleless. It can be used to synonymously express the following "not one of us," "wretch," "unknown," "other," or "demon," Nawga is universally recognized by all members comprising the scaled races. It is the highest insult, offense and disgrace in reptilian societies. It is used as a derogatory to address the other, an unscaled individual, a "not a" that is not us.

Dragon culture

Dra-kin

Meaning; dragon kin. A term of affiliation that is used by dragons in addressing members of their race.

Topography guide for the diverse land masses and structures of Aråb-Duele

The planet Aråb-Duele: was ravaged by a billion-year war that destroyed 85% of its biodiversity and made 80% of its flora and fauna become extinct. In addition, all of the water and moisture on this planet—with the exception of the mudlands—has been replaced with an arid, dry landscape comprised of lava, rock and krystal.
Note: *krystal refers to crystal, but the c is swapped with a k.*

Basacoirisha: is a continent consisting of a chain of massive active volcanoes, they house a major city, Caldor. On the fringes and edges of Basacoirisha are smaller, yet still active volcanoes that surround the landmass in all directions and climb up further north, where the second major city Calanth-Uwell is.

Clay/hard earth/stone: comprises a majority of the surface of the world. If the ground does not give way to desert or mudlands then it is hard, rough stone and hard-packed clay.

Deserts: comprise over 80% of the world's mass. The continents and landmasses have developed around them.

The Emerald Lands: are overlapping ridges made from emerald. The ridges intersect and interlock like infinite fingers that are intertwined. Their texture is jagged. The Emerald Lands are a continent that levitates hundreds of thousands of miles above the encircling mudlands and quicksand below it.

The Iron Lands: are a massive continent made of iron. 95% of its landmass is underground, with a small portion of it emerging through the ground like the bow of a massive ship. The part that is visible on land is hundreds of miles across and tall like a massive mountain.

Krystal: is a staple on this planet. Many landmasses such as mountains and canyons are made from it. All plants/flora are composed of krystal. There are no flora composed of biological matter. Krystal as a texture is ragged, ridged and full of spiky growths.

Krystal ridges/trees: are very tall structures that are faceted and full of ridges. These grow in clusters like trees in a forest and can grow in such large groups that they comprise an entire valley. Some valleys are entirely made up of these structures/growths. Krystal ridges can also grow in forests spanning hundreds of miles.

The Metal Lands: are a series of three concentric steel triangular landmasses composed of steel ridges. Within the center of the Metal Lands is a volcano and underneath it is a secret subterranean city, Tstsubasa.

Molten lava rivers and lakes: are bodies of molten lava that have been pushed up from below the surface of the planet and have carved out the land over billions of years. These bodies of lava cover a large percentage of the planet's surface.

Mountains and canyons: are land forms composed of either three materials, stone, krystal or metal. Stone serving as the default substance for geological considerations does not warrant an explanation. There are various types of metals that mountains are composed of such as gold, bronze, copper or silver, as well as krystal. There are different shades and colors of krystal, grades so to speak. Red, pink, green, etc. The mountains that are made of metal are formed of different materials, since each metal has a different texture and chemical composition.

Mudlands/quicksand: are large bodies of mud/mire that can be found in different parts of the world, spanning for hundreds of miles on different continents. This mud is often thick and slushy with the consistency of cement before it hardens.

Plants/trees/forests: are the flora of this world and are entirely made of krystal. The leaves in the forests are composed of fire and eternally blaze.

Obsidian ridges: are overgrown, protruding, jagged, splintered and fractured shards of obsidian that surround the mainland continent of Vreishri' Gaael for thousands upon thousands of miles and grow in a wall thousands upon thousands of miles high. The ridges are like a massive spiky bulwark full of infinite shards, many the size of individual mountains.

Suns: are celestial bodies of which there are five that this world orbits. Four rise and set in the four primary directions; North, East, South, West and the fifth that moves perpendicular to the rest. All the suns rise and set daily.

Acknowledgments

A lot of people can go into the production of a book, sometimes it's just a key few. I want to thank all of you. First and foremost, I want to thank my parents. Their infinite support since I started drafting this, back in tenth grade when I was fifteen years old, up until now. To my mom, who enjoyed hearing many of the life-changing moments Zammus went through, and to my dad, who was the first person to hear the title of book 1 and the name of this series. I remember the pure exhilaration, joy and overall excitement of calling you that morning and how absolutely thrilled you were. And to my older sis, Lia, for that one time, or maybe it was twice, where she and her friend listened to me read an excerpt and she thought it was pretty cool and genuinely interesting.

To Urga, my endearing partner. For all the countless support and encouragement you give me on a daily basis with all the constant tasks I juggle: the amount is truly insane. I appreciate all the emotional stability you provide through it all.

Special devoted thanks to my dear brother, Andrew. We've had dozens of several hour-long phone calls and laughs over the many years about the mythos and characters of this world, particularly "that" hilarious, epic and iconic moment that's become our greatest inside joke of the entire series and a meme for us at this point! Man, I hope that moment goes viral one of these days: if so the world won't be ready! Next is my other brother, dearest Oscar. You've always been a real one, man.

You have my infinite gratitude and respect for being willing to actually beta read the entire 930 page story from cover to cover and to have partaken in very profound and meaningful conversations, analyzing all the plot points and characters with me and answering my relentless questions! Thank you, brother!

My editing friend, Nicole Alyssa, who connected to me to Timothy J. Gonzales; Myths and Maps; the legend! Tim, you've spent the most time co-developing my world. Since working on my maps back in spring 2023 to now, we've become the best of brothers. I can't say how much I have genuinely appreciated all your advice and book launch suggestions, talking all things writing and world-building. It's because of you that this book is out here now: without that big talk we had I'd still only be working on book 2 and this story would still be on the shelf! Without you, there would be no maps, chapter icons, part illustrations or cover. From the beginning up to now you've overperformed and contributed over a billion percent of effort in everything you've done. Your attitude, friendship, insights, professionalism and craftsmanship. Every conversation has been stellar and beyond fun! Your witty, personable adventurous spirit ties it all together! You truly did it all and took me from zero to hero! You're the real MVP here! Thank you, my man!

"JSK" Jennifer Schomburg Kanke, my creative writing teacher from college, who has stayed in touch throughout the years and been a support line to discuss all things writing and who has seen me grow. Thank you for introducing me to your editor friend, Kate Lechler. Kate, my manuscript would not have gotten to where it is now without your line edits, you cleaned it up and showed me my blind spots.

My wonderful formatter, Niels Schoenmaker, without Tim I wouldn't have found you. I appreciated your positive upbeat enthusiasm from the get-go. I can't thank you enough for your incredibly thorough and meticulous attention to detail and all the inconsistencies that you espied with your discerning gaze. I could not have run the manuscript under the razor like you did even if I wanted to! Aside from your endless vigilance, I also want to thank you for your ever-present candor, camaraderie and wonderful attitude.

Raazol, I love talking philosophy and sci-fi fantasy world-building with you. Our first great epic discourse was discussing "His Dark Materials." You, sir, are a true treasure, keep on writing Philosopher King! Lastly, my other writing brother from across the world who I keep up with on the weekly: "Jon," Jonathan Besanko, this one is for you. From all the discussions we've had about dragons, mythology, TV shows, horror, historical epics, Nordic, Japanese, Germanic and Babylonian folklore and literature and the plethora of world-creation myths and legends to all things comics. You're a living legend and massive inspiration to me, bro. Keep on getting published!

And lastly to you, dear reader. Thanks for giving a new author a chance.

Sneak Peek

Volume Two of Book One
of
The Anura Chronicles

17

Luxurious Escort; What Sheer Convenience Can Afford

"Reszch-Sploisha-Tor!"

Those words of sorcery hit me like arrows made of lead. I was thrown off the ground, my staff hurled from my hands and I came to a halt suspended in midair like a frozen water droplet. My assailants revealed themselves as none other than the two prugalas. One was tall and both were sinewy, lacking the robustness of their leader. They had brown flaky scales the color of dead leaves and wasted refuse. They both possessed sickly yellow eyes. One had a black zigzagging scar that split its face in two from brow to chin. Its shorter companion walked with a hunch and favored its weight on its left leg. Its tattered cowl hid its face and, from where I floated, I could see that it was missing some fingers on both its hands. The one with the scar came towards me and clucked its tongue. I dropped face first onto the ground.

Panting, I rolled over, looking around me. Murgen wasn't holding her own that well. Their dragon was blasting her every couple of yards with glowing purple ring-shaped outbursts of air that it discharged from its helmet and the discs on its body.

"What are you?" the scar-faced prugala demanded, standing above me.

"It's not an auríl. Not the way it changed like that!" its companion spat, growling and grunting as it stepped beside it.

"Don't matter much, Quore. Not after I sink this into it," the same prugala snarled as a pillar of sand flowed up from the ground and into its hand. In seconds the stream of grains solidified into a savage, curving sword.

Though it's sand, I have no doubt that he can keep it solid enough to pass through my stone body. If only the staff would protect me right now. Death isn't certain, but isn't it clearly imminent enough? Ahhhh, I agonized.

"I could melt you into magma right now!" the sorcerer called Quore barked. He screamed out something unintelligible and a green detonating blast hammered into me, flipping me through the air and head on into a flying, spinning Murgen.

"Aghhhuhhh!" we both screamed painfully from the impact.

"Great timing!" The dragon applauded.

"Blast them with a triple, gang! We won't kill them. Not yet, but still!" Shenrai grinned.

"Whatever and however you say it, boss!" his cronies replied.

"It's been so long, too long since we've performed the triangle!" The dragon laughed gleefully as it and the other two prugalas spread out in three different directions.

"Been too long, Holdzar!" Quore agreed, smirking and grinning at his fellow prugala.

The air changed as the two prugalas and dragon enlarged the triangle. Without shame I gripped Murgen's hand in fear. She glared at me but didn't let go. Grains of sand began leaving the ground and floating upward as three rays of light were birthed from our assailants: one yellow, bright purple, and jade green. The three spears of light hit us all at once, blinding me. Murgen howled out a scream. Everything disappeared. Infinite blackness descended.

***

I juddered awake. It was dark and I was immediately aware of the bonds winding me from shoulder to ankle. There was a green bonfire before me. *Isn't this familiar,* my mind chuckled, thinking back to my initial encounter with Dar Vagoue.

"Hmph," Murgen remarked as she observed me from across the flames.

The emerald flames were about two meters high, but I could still make out her shape. Like me she was sitting with her body at a right angle, tied up, and propped up against a stone. Spread out around the cabbage-shaped fire were our captors. Shenrai was pacing, a broad and ferocious dagger in his hands. The dragon was watching me intently, the remnants of its gear having been removed from its body. The emerald flames were reflecting beautifully off its navy-blue scales, giving them a purplish silver-white iridescent hue. The flames also highlighted the fresh purple scabs on its shoulders from our battle earlier and made them appear as a ghastly, rotting brown.

"You've changed, friend," it intoned, speaking directly to me.

"What?" I mumbled, still shocked, dazed and confused.

"Your skin," it replied. "Look."

My eyes dove to my hand, chest, and legs. They were the brown of my flesh where the stone had not yet crept in. I looked back at the dragon.

"You must now be wondering why I told you. I want you to understand the full scope of your situation," it chuckled in its throat. "What are you? You're not auríl. Where do you come from?"

Auríl. What is that? That is the second or third time I've heard that. And the second time today. Is that a race? One of the six? I pondered, looking down and studying my bonds.

They consisted of two types of cord, the thicker one made of sorcerously-hardened sand while the other was formed of translucent cables of sorcerous energy. Beads of sweat were gathering on the flesh of my face. Something leathery and bark-like clubbed my face, jerking it left and drawing liquid fire from my right cheek.

"Vluthe here asked you a question!" hissed a prugala standing above me. "Do I have to hit you again?" it barked, raising its long-fingered hand.

I flinched away, breathing hard. My chest felt something long, narrow and sharp glide across it. Heart hammering, I watched the dragon circle the small barb on the tip of its tail over my stoned shoulder.

"Now, now," it gloated, purring deeply. "Listen to my friend Holdzar. And I promise just a quick prick," the dragon beseeched, staring directly into my eyes. With a swift *twunk!*

it pierced my shoulder, twisted shallowly into the flesh, and cleanly ejected itself.

"AghhhHHH!" I gasped as molten lava flowed slowly.

"It bleeds like us! Wait! Is that lava blood?!" the dragon barked aghast.

"Let's draw more!" the prugala grinned.

"Or . . . ," came a new voice.

A foot collided with my stomach with incredibly unbelievable force.

"Do that!" the voice finished.

My back arched as I flew backwards into darkness, all the air in my body void.

Prugalas, five to seven to twelve times stronger than you, Jaow-kieen's voice reminded me.

My back came crashing down tremendously hard on pebbles. Grimacing, gritting my teeth, and sighing, I cried inwardly, *Ahhh, when does it end? Will it end? Is there such a thing?*

Voices yelled from where the fire was, "Boss! Can we kill it yet?"

I was numb to Shenrai's answer.

"Yes. I couldn't care less! As long as it's in front of me when you do!"

"Bring it back here, Quore!" someone that had to be either Vluthe or Holdzar yelled.

In less than a moment two scaly hands picked me up like a sack of potatoes.

"Hope you like flying," he whispered, grinning into my ear.

In what felt effortless my carrier propelled me away from him and I was soaring the last three or four yards towards the fire.

Not in the fire! Not in the fire! Not in the fire! my mind squealed. *Change! To stone! Protect yourself! You need your armor! Change! Now!* it commanded.

My skin refused to shake and quiver.

Can't! I can't! No! Not in the fire! I yelped.

Strong robust arms stopped me, catching me. Mere inches from the flames

"Let it watch Murgen die. Then we can destroy it!" Shenrai grinned, depositing me facedown next to Murgen.

"Murgen!" He gave her a mighty kick that drew a gasp from her lips and flipped her onto her back. "Quore! The blade!" he said, handing a huge cleaver to his sorcerer.

"Master," his sycophant purred, as he fervently held the weapon he whispered a quick prayer over the blade and passed it back to Shenrai.

I immediately felt an intense wave of heat like the intensity of dragon fire.

"Make it watch! Prop it up!" Shenrai spoke softly.

One of the sorcerers–I couldn't tell which–grabbed me by both arms and forced me to my knees. The blade in Shenrai's right hand was easily longer than my arm and bathed in blazing blinding flames that kept changing from emerald, to blue, to white.

"Murgen! As lord and leader of the Torns't Company of Bounty Hunters, I sentence you to death! All in favor proclaim! All against proclaim!" Shenrai bellowed.

"Death! Death! Death! What she deserves!" his companions yelled in ecstasy.

"Hmmm. The chorus has allowed its approval and vented its permission! Shall she be allowed to confess her crimes?!" he demanded.

"No! No! No! She's not worthy of her own defense or anyone's for that matter!" his audience decreed.

"They have spoken! You aren't at all well liked, Murgen!" he grinned, snarling at her. "For thirty-three years you were with us. We were your brothers! Sworn to you and you to us. And you betrayed us! Our limitless faithfulness and impossible loyalties!" he roared.

"Hear! Hear! Hear!" his cronies yelled back.

"You know our oaths! You swore them before us all. In the presence of your brothers; Vluthe, Holdzar, Quore, and I, Shenrai! I hereby now sentence you on account of death for your desertion!" he thundered.

"Hear! Hear! Hear!" his goons boomed back.

He hacked, swinging the fire-possessed blade down towards her neck. A surprised intake of breath passed through his body. The blade clattered to the stones as a pike tore through his chest, launching him many yards away. Another shaft ripped through a sorcerer and threw him within the emerald fire. Before I could blink, another shot through the last prugala, taking his head clean off. Before the dragon could react, two huge projectiles raced through it, one in the chest that came out the back and the other in its skull. The body of the headless prugala fell, crumpling to the ground. The shafts that ended the dragon were huge; each must have been as wide as a mast.

Four riders trotted into our line of sight. Their steeds were the stone creatures we had seen earlier, before Shenrai's ambush. Parfins. Six huge, impossibly stocky men of average height also appeared, walking behind them. The lead rider approached. He was garbed simply. He wore black trousers that reflected green from the emerald flames and a gray cape of a seemingly thin and light material that rustled as he moved. His feet and torso were bare. Black streams that looked like tar grew on his head. His forearms were sheathed in gray bulky vambraces; each housed a small sapphire. His eyes were completely blue, with no pupil or iris, a light sky blue like the creature I became when I turned.

Bellowing he cried, "Murgen of House Mononoke, daughter of King Aradŭr and Queen Hoysa, sworn to House Narayum! We are here to escort you back to the kingdom under the authority of their most royal and honorable graces, our king and queen!"

"Thank you. But what?" Murgen gasped, completely bewildered and shocked.

"My Princess," the rider had stepped off his mount and was offering his hand to her, "I am Captain and Commander Yoren of the First Legion. I was at your birth all those decades ago," he spoke in a calm, steady, kind, and deep voice.

Everyone in his company was made of stone in varying shades of white through gray.

And now what happens to me? I thought, pondering the unknown hands of fate.

"It's about time, I suppose, to go home. And I suppose I don't really have a choice," Murgen replied coolly, refusing his hand with a sneer and distancing herself from the captain.

With a quiet swiftness and masterful subtlety, a threadbare blue string slithered into existence on the ground beside my hands and wound itself around my left wrist. *Hopefully it's too dark for anyone to have noticed,* I thought. I dared not move, the last thing I needed was to appear threatening.

"Sir!" someone bellowed. "What do we do with this thing?"

My eyes darted around. A sea of cold blue eyes was surrounding me, every one of them prying, attempting to judge and ascertain my level of depth.

"It's got stone!" a soldier barked.

"It is of stone!" another observed.

"What is it?" another called from the back of a parfin.

Will they kill me? I thought to myself.

"I don't know," I whispered.

Will she have them kill me? Will she let them? I questioned.

"I don't know," I whispered.

The commander walked towards me, drawing a wide bone-white sword from his right hip.

"Indeed," he intoned, standing above me. "What are you and where do you come from? And how did this happen?"

With the word "this" he pointed with his sword at my stomach, gesturing to the parts of my body that were still of human flesh. Unlike my shoulders, parts of my upper back, the inner parts of my thighs, my fingers, elbows, and half of my right foot that had been replaced by the stone. I gulped, exchanging glances with Murgen.

"I was born as one of stone. You all can see the stone on me. That is me. Years ago, I was cursed by a prugala sorcerer who afflicted my body with these fleshy growths, here, here and here," I said touching the skin on my face, stomach, arms and legs. "I found and killed him a fortnight ago. That was the only way to break the curse, he told me himself as my blade sat in his throat. Since then, the damage has been reversing itself. More of the stone grows back over my body as this fleshy disease goes away. Take me and in time you will see that flesh will no longer pollute me and that only stone will rule me. As it is meant to and as it should for us all," I finished.

"Hmmm," the commander mumbled, "I can't not acknowledge the parts of you that are stone. However, tell me this; what are you doing traveling with the Princess? And if I don't like your answer, your neck will have to meet my sword," he spoke.

I eyed Murgen for a moment. "She found me in a desert. I was alone. As was she," I replied, well aware that if she betrayed me and told the full truth about the creature and it turning into me during the fight I'd be dead.

"Is this true, Princess?" the commander asked.

My brown eyes pleaded into the green and orange worlds of Murgen's.

Please! Don't say it! my mind begged.

Formless blades of anxiety ripped open and through my stomach.

Her answer was a full-fledged cannonball to my chest.

Olin and Milou Photography

SAMUEL A. ZAMOR was born in the vibrant, tropical cultural art scene of Miami, Florida. He found his calling when he was six years old penning story books on the floor in his room and has been writing ever since. He graduated from Florida State University with a degree in Editing Writing Media and got his post-graduate in Technical Writing at Algonquin College in Ottawa, Canada. When Samuel isn't writing he is often conversing with his retinue of dragons debating matters of sorcery and quantum physics, studying military history, hiking, playing guitar, reading comics and building Gundam models and Metal Earth Kits. He lives with his partner in California. To keep up with his book updates, follow his instagram *@sam.zamor*.

Made in the USA
Monee, IL
09 August 2025

22094806R00146